To Austin,

Happy Hauntings!

The Ghosts of Malhado

Also by H. J. Ralles

The Keeper Series

Keeper of the Kingdom
Keeper of the Realm
Keeper of the Empire
Keeper of the Colony
Keeper of the Island

The Darok Series

Darok 9
Darok 10

The Curse of Charron

www.hjralles.com

The Ghosts of Malhado

By

H. J. Ralles

Top Publications Ltd.
Dallas, Texas.

The Ghosts of Malhado

A Top Publications Paperback
First Edition

12221 Merit Drive, Suite 950
Dallas, Texas 75251

Hardback ISBN 978-1-929976-83-6
Paperback ISBN 978-1-929976-80-5
Library of Congress 2011926038

The characters and events in this novel are fictional and created out of the imagination of the author. Certain real locations and institutions are mentioned, but the characters and events depicted are entirely fictional.

For

Suzan Assiter Zachariah

A Realtor in a million

Acknowledgements

I would like to thank the wonderful people of Brazoria County, Texas for their help in writing this book. In particular, I would like to thank: Suzan Zachariah, who inspired me to write the story during our house-hunting expeditions and then sent me countless snippets of valuable information; Michael Bailey and Jamie Murray of the Brazoria County Historical Museum; James Glover, Brazoria County Parks Department; Debbie Broadway, Manager of Bright Lite, San Luis Pass; the Village of Surfside Beach Museum; and David Devaney, who wrote the wonderful poem on the last page of this book. Finally, I would like to thank Fannie Mae Follett Gilbert, who willingly shared her family history.

I am truly honored to be part of the beautiful community of Treasure Island in San Luis Pass, where the residents have built and rebuilt after every hurricane. This community draws its hope and courage from the Folletts, who rebuilt Half Way House after the huge storm of 1883, from Mr. Bright who rebuilt the Bright Lite after Alicia in 1983, and now from those who have recently rebuilt after Ike in 2008 . . . and all of those storms in between.

Bright is the light of Malhado!

Malhado

Oh Malhado, Malhado,
My San Luis Isle
Holds history's secrets
All this while,
Buried on Malhado

Storm after storm
Beats on your shore,
Washes away
Our houses for sure,
But still we return.

Oh Malhado, Malhado,
My San Luis Isle,
Sandy beaches
Mile after mile,
What befalls you now?

Year after year,
Tide after tide,
You'll last the ages
To show with pride,
That bright is the light of Malhado.

H.J. Ralles

Part 1

The Ghosts
of
Malhado

Chapter 1

"Malhado!"

Alex looked over his shoulder to see who was calling, but no one was there. He listened intently, but all he could hear was the sound of the waves crashing on the beach. *I must have been imagining it,* he thought. He turned his attention back to the small sand dollar in his hand—it was almost perfect. What a beauty! It would make a great addition to his collection, for sure.

"Malhado!"

There it was again—the same sorrowful three-note call, like a whisper in the wind. Alex spun around and scoured the dunes. The only movement was from the sand kicked up in the sea breeze. The sun sinking over Christmas Bay set the sky ablaze with streaks of reds and yellows. While beautiful, it warned of impending darkness.

1

Suddenly Alex felt quite alone. The beach was now deserted. He looked at his watch — it was past 8 o'clock! He was supposed to have been back at the beach house an hour ago! His mom had allowed him to stay behind while she prepared dinner, but once again he had lost track of time waiting eagerly to see what treasures were brought in by the ebbing tide. She would be furious.

Alex raced along the water's edge toward the lights of the houses in Treasure Island, but as he approached the little bridge over the dunes there was a bright flash of red light, then a flash of blue. He stopped dead in his tracks, blinded for a second.

The sand dollar fell from his hand.

"Ahhhh!" he screamed. Now he was seeing things too!

A man in a strange costume with a funny-looking metal hat was standing on the bridge, blocking his path to Jolly Roger Road. And his face . . . what was up with his face? He didn't have a nose! His sunken eyes were haunting, as if the life had been sucked right out of them, and his teeth had a strange blue tinge. The light from the street behind him seemed to pass right though his body! How could that be?

Alex rubbed his eyes. Dare he look again? He opened one eye and then the other. The man was still there—but now with a cutlass drawn! He started to march on the bridge, but his big black boots made no sound at all. And instead of moving towards Alex, the man started to rise in the air!

"Malhado! Malhado!" the man wailed, hovering just in front of Alex's head. He sliced his cutlass through the air, making a frightening whooshing sound.

Alex covered his head with his hands, terrified that he was about to be cut to shreds. He wanted to run but he couldn't move. It was as if someone had glued him to the spot. "Who . . . who . . . who are you?" he stammered.

The man's soft response seemed to encircle Alex, forcing him to listen.

"Malhado, my Malhado,
My heart is full of sorrow
Such a heavy loss I bear
Of flesh *and* treasure, be aware
I cannot rest! I cannot go!
While 'tis buried on Malhado."

"W. . . w . . .what does that mean?" Alex asked.

"'Tis buried on Malhado," the man repeated, his voice trailing off into the wind. And then, with a wave of his cutlass and another flash of red light, he was gone.

Alex could feel his heart pounding. His hands were clammy, his legs were like jelly and the sea air now seemed to have a dank smell. Did he really just see and hear a ghost? No! Of course not! He didn't believe in such things, and besides, ghosts can't speak . . . can they?

Alex drew in a deep breath. His brain must be playing tricks on him. He'd been staring at the sand looking for shells far too long. Yes, that was it, for sure. He laughed out loud in an effort to convince himself, and walked straight up to the little bridge. It still took all the bravery he could muster to place his right foot on the first wooden plank, and then his left on the second. Then slowly he took two more steps.

He picked up the pace, laughing at his own stupidity. "Ghosts? How dumb!" What was he thinking? But as he reached the center of the bridge his head started spinning and his stomach churned. He grabbed for the wooden handrail, certain he was going to throw up. The dunes faded in and out of his vision and became a blur of sea and sky. The bridge swayed under his feet.

"Ahhhh!" he screamed. "Someone help meeeeee. . . pleeease!"

The bridge shook violently. They didn't have earthquakes in Texas, did they? It was as if he were falling through the sky, down and down and down.

"Oh, Malhado, Malhado . . . 'tis buried on Malhado," he heard as his arms flailed madly in the air.

Alex landed on his back with a thud. "Ouch!" His back ached and his head pounded. He groaned in agony. Now he really regretted spending all day with his head down searching for shells. His mother had warned him about sunstroke. Next time he'd put a towel over his neck and be sure to leave the beach with everyone else.

Slowly he moved his legs, and then his arms. "Better get back to the beach house," he muttered, standing up slowly.

He grabbed for the handrail of the bridge to steady himself—but it wasn't there! In fact, the bridge wasn't there! His heart began to race as he looked around. He was still on the beach, for sure, but wait . . . it didn't look the same! Trees . . . there were trees where there hadn't been any before! The dunes were much higher, the beach was wider, and all around him the tall grasses danced madly in the sea breeze. And where were the lights from the houses of Treasure Island? The only light came from the sun, which was just rising above the horizon.

What had happened? Wasn't it evening, not dawn? Wasn't he on his way back to the beach house for the night?

Now he was panic struck.

Chapter 2

Alex rubbed his forehead, trying to figure out what had happened. Had the fall on the bridge knocked him unconscious? That could explain why he couldn't remember a whole night, but it didn't explain the change of scenery and the disappearance of the bridge. Or was he hallucinating?

Of course! That must be it. The fall must have been worse than he thought. The bridge was probably still there but he just wasn't seeing it. "Gotta get back to the beach house. Mom will know what to do, for sure."

He staggered along the beach close to the water, hoping that he was going in the right direction. The Gulf of Mexico suddenly seemed rough and the waves lashed on the shore. He could feel the spray on his face, but he didn't much mind. He loved the sea. He looked for the familiar houses across the San Luis Pass on Galveston Island, but then felt miserable when he couldn't see them. Galveston looked strangely deserted.

He stopped. What was that riding in on the crest of a wave? "Not again!" shouted Alex. "What am I seeing now?"

He watched in disbelief as a small boat was hurled in the air by a huge wave and cast upon the beach. It landed with a loud crash and a shudder. Men appeared from the bottom of the boat, like ants crawling out of a Texas fire ant mound. They dragged themselves over the sides and collapsed on the sand, wet and bedraggled. Many more threw themselves over the bow and then crawled on all fours up the beach before falling on their bellies. Alex counted over thirty men lying on the sand, many of whom looked almost dead.

Alex's boy-scout training took over. He forgot his fear and his pain and, without thinking of the consequences, ran down the beach waving his arms and shouting, "Are you all okay? Do you need help?"

Not one of the men responded. In fact, not one of the men seemed to see him! He didn't get it—even though it was just dawn he could see them in this light, so why couldn't they see him? Alex stood there dumbfounded. He bent over a large man who lay on his back, groaning. "Sir! Sir! Are you hurt?" he asked.

The man sat up and turned to one of his companions. "*Luz un incendio,*" he ordered.

"Spanish! You're speaking Spanish!" said Alex excitedly. "*Estás hablando español.* I've been learning Spanish in school. You just said 'Light a fire' so you must be okay!" But still they ignored him. "What is *wrong* with you all?" he finally screamed. But not one of the men so much as turned his head to look at him.

Alex was shaking as he watched three of the men clamber to their feet and start to gather driftwood. Now it seemed that *he* was the ghost! They didn't hear him and they certainly didn't see him! In fact, they staggered back and forth right past him, as if he weren't even there. He was totally confused. Surrounded by waving grasses, he sat down a short way back from the group, tears welling in his eyes. What should he do? What *could* he do? It seemed to him that his only option was to sit and watch.

The fire was soon lit. The men tried to warm themselves—their soaking wet garments clung to their bodies and were covered in sand. Alex stared at their clothing. It was unlike anything he had seen before, except in history books—baggy pleated pants gathered above the knees, and long-sleeved shirts with fancy cuffs.

He listened carefully and found he could pick up some of the Spanish from their conversation. Maybe now he would figure out who these men were and what had happened. The one who had instructed the other man to light a fire seemed to be in command. He said to his men, "It is the sixth of the month of November."

"No, it's not!" shouted Alex. "It's June 16th! It's the beginning of my summer vacation!"

"Lope, climb to the top of one of those trees. Take a look around and see where we are," ordered the man.

A few minutes later Lope shouted from the treetop, "Vaca, we're on an island."

Alex sat up straighter. That wasn't right! Treasure Island might be called an island, but it certainly wasn't one! It was just a little neighborhood at the tip of Follett's Island . . . but could Lope see the whole of Follett's Island from the top of the tree? Alex doubted it.

Lope then disappeared down a worn path through the grass on the orders of Vaca. Alex watched him go, and then looked back at the men lying by the fire. Some of them were still shivering in wet clothing and others looked so sick and injured that he wondered if they would die before his eyes. Thank goodness the sun was up, as Alex was also feeling cold. He wasn't sure if it was the weather or because he didn't feel well.

He didn't have long to think about it when there were shouts from along the beach. Lope was running back towards the group, breathlessly screaming, "Indians! Indians!"

Instinctively Alex lowered himself in the grass. The Spanish explorers could not see him, but perhaps the Indians could. He dared not risk it. Even after everything that had happened, at least he was alive.

One by one, the Indians slowly appeared from behind the trees. They walked in one long line along the beach towards the Spaniards.

Only a few of the men around the fire staggered to their feet. The others looked totally defeated, as if they had accepted death by bow and arrow.

Alex's heart was racing. What would happen? Would the Indians kill the Spaniards? He stared over the grass, almost too scared to watch. There must have been one hundred Indian archers gathered on the beach. They were tall and muscular, and their bottom lips were pierced with thin pieces of cane. The Spaniards had no weapons of any description. How could they defend themselves?

Vaca was already on his feet, bravely walking towards the Indians, flanked by two of his men. Their arms were raised to show that they were unarmed.

The chief, distinguishable by his headdress of feathers, placed his bow and arrow on the sand and moved forward with two others to greet Vaca and his men. The two groups stood looking at each other for what seemed an age. Alex held his breath.

Vaca's companions took beads from around their necks and gave them to the Indians, whose faces showed instant delight at the gifts. Everyone seemed to relax a little. Vaca lowered his arms and slowly reached inside the top of his shirt. He grasped a cord around his neck and yanked off a leather pouch, which he then proceeded to open. He tipped something into his hand. What was it?

Then, as if Vaca had heard Alex's thoughts, he held up a beautiful necklace of small, gleaming, dark blue stones. They twinkled in the morning sun as he turned the necklace in different directions for all to see. Alex gasped. Were they sapphires?

The Indians began to whoop and holler. Even Vaca's men gaped and looked closer, as if they had no prior knowledge of Vaca's valuable possession.

Vaca undid the clasp and placed the dazzling prize around the chief's neck. The chief fingered the jewelry, smiling broadly, and then turned and picked up one of his arrows. He placed it carefully in Vaca's open hands. A lot of bowing of heads followed, and both sides used hand signals in an effort to communicate. Finally, the chief led his men away, still fingering his proud acquisition as he walked along the beach.

Alex let out a deep breath. What had he just witnessed? It was something quite amazing, for sure. He lay back on the dunes, replaying the scene in his mind and watching the grasses waving all around him. They were mesmerizing.

* * * * *

Alex heard sea birds. He opened one eye and then the other, squinting to see in the glaring light. The sun was straight above him. He looked from side to side, and realized he was still on the beach. He must have fallen asleep on the dunes for an hour or two.

He sat up just in time to witness Vaca skulking off from the group. He was trudging along the beach and heading in the direction of San Luis Pass. The rest of the

Spaniards were asleep by the fire, probably still exhausted from their ordeal.

"Where's he going on his own?" muttered Alex.

He watched Vaca for a minute, and then finally gave in to his curiosity and followed him. It was tough to walk on the heavy shell beach. His feet seemed to sink deeper and deeper with every step, filling his shoes with bits of shell and sand.

Alex followed Vaca round the point. On this side of the island the sea looked even rougher. Gone was the lovely sapphire blue that Alex admired on a calm day. Instead the ocean looked emerald green, which usually meant that threatening weather wasn't far behind. It was nearly high tide, and the narrow strip of beach was littered with slimy oyster shells. His shoes were wet and it became hard to even stay upright on the treacherous surface. The waves crashed around him, water sometimes swirling above his knees.

The beach suddenly dropped off at a steep angle. Alex had heard that several people had died here — sucked under by the strong flow of San Luis Pass. How lucky Vaca and his men had been to have landed farther down the beach. If they had been tossed ashore here, all would likely have drowned.

Vaca trudged up the beach into the dunes and out of reach of the huge waves. Then he removed his shirt and spread it out on the sand. What *was* the man up to?

Alex stared in disbelief. "No way! It couldn't be!" Hanging from Vaca's neck was another small brown pouch! Alex instantly wondered if it contained something as beautiful as the necklace he had given the Indian chief that morning. It would make sense if he had kept even more valuable things for himself. He watched, hoping Vaca would once again reveal its contents.

Vaca knelt down and began to scoop away the sand with his bare hands. Alex strained to see what he was doing.

"Aww! Don't do that to me!" moaned Alex, as Vaca quickly wrapped the pouch up in his shirt and stuffed it down in the hole he had dug. "I want to know what's in the pouch!" Then Vaca piled sand in a huge mound on top and patted it down.

"Now what's he doing?" said Alex. "Man, he's collecting shells!" Vaca gathered an armful of oyster shells and piled them on top of the mound, marking the place where he had buried his pouch.

Even though Vaca couldn't see him, Alex decided to wait until he had gone before walking closer. Perhaps he would even uncover the pouch and take a look. How thrilling! This was like hunting for buried treasure. After all, his beach house *was* in Treasure Island!

Vaca scrambled back along the beach, occasionally looking back over his shoulder as if he were trying to remember the location of his hiding place. Alex was dying with excitement, hardly able to contain himself as Vaca passed him.

Suddenly a large wave crashed over Alex's head, knocking him down. He fought to stand upright but his feet couldn't grip the surface. He clawed with his nails into the shells on the beach, but the sand seemed to slip through his fingers as he was dragged back into the water. He tried to breathe, but found himself swallowing salty water instead.

His heart beat faster. *Get up, Alex! Get yourself up!* he told himself. *You could drown!* Even for a good swimmer, the rip currents were strong in San Luis Pass.

Alex coughed and spluttered and struggled harder to stand. No matter what he did, the ocean sucked him farther and farther back into its depths. Now his heart was racing and he felt dizzy with panic.

He desperately tried to get a foothold once again, but just as he managed to stand up and scream, "Help!" another huge wave crashed over his head, knocking him down again. He just couldn't stay above the water! He thrashed his arms, trying to stay upright, but the currents kept pulling him under.

Sea water filled his lungs. Now he was choking, fighting desperately to breathe. His head was spinning. His arms ached and his legs couldn't fight anymore. He couldn't do anything! He couldn't save himself!

Fear engulfed him.

Mom! Dad! Help me! Where were they? Would he ever see them again?

Another monster wave roared in, throwing his body hard against the bottom. Alex was lost beneath the sea.

Chapter 3

"Malhado! Malhado!" Alex groaned.

"Alex! Alex! You're okay!"

Alex's head pounded and he instinctively touched behind his ear. "Oww! That hurts!"

"Don't touch, Alex! Lie still. You've had a really bad fall. You've got a deep gash across the back of your head and bruises everywhere."

"Mom? Is that you?" Slowly he opened his eyes and tried to focus. Everything was a blur, but he could just make out the tall slender form of his mother leaning over him. He tried to sit up, but his head throbbed.

"Lie down, Alex. You need to rest," she said, gently pushing him back against the pillow. "Besides, you've got to sit up slowly—you're on the bottom bunk. You don't want to hit your head again, do you? Isn't once enough for this vacation?" She said it with a slight laugh, but Alex could tell by her tone that it wasn't meant as a joke.

"The bottom bunk? I'm at our beach house?"

"Yes, you're safely back at Island Sapphire."

"How did you rescue me from the sea?"

"The sea? You weren't *in* the sea, Alex." His mom paused. "You were lying unconscious on the beach. Your dad found you in the dark by the side of the footbridge. We had to call an ambulance and get you to the hospital in Galveston. We were all so worried . . . you have no idea!"

"Hospital? I went to hospital?"

"We took you to the ER. The doctor sewed you up—you've got ten stitches! He said you had sunstroke and a bad concussion too. You must have fallen over the handrail of the little footbridge on your way back here. Just how you did that, I really don't know! But then I *never* know with you!"

It was true—he was *always* injuring himself. "But the ghost . . . and the Indians . . ."

"Don't try to talk, dear. The doctor says you've got to rest, and then you'll be as good as new in a few days. I'll get you some juice and I'll be right back."

"But Mom . . ." She disappeared through the door, leaving it ajar.

Alex stared at the bottom of the upper bunk, hardly daring to turn his head in any direction—it thumped so hard. It was summer vacation—June, wasn't it? "That's right, it's June and I've just finished sixth grade," he mumbled to himself.

Now he remembered. They were staying at Island Sapphire, their beach house, for two weeks. How he loved it here!

It was a sky blue beach house, in the heart of the neighborhood of Treasure Island in San Luis Pass, Texas. His family had built Island Sapphire soon after Hurricane Ike ravaged the Gulf Coast. It was built sixteen feet off the ground to protect the house from flooding during hurricanes. Not only did it have a huge deck both at the back and at the front on the first level, but it also had decks at both ends on the second level!

The views from the top floor were spectacular. Alex loved to watch the Gulf waves crashing on the shore, and then run across to the deck on the other side and watch the sunset over Cold Pass and Christmas Bay. But best of all, the house was only a two-minute walk to the most awesome beach ever.

Now his eyes were focusing better and he could think more clearly. He turned his head slightly to look at the bunkroom he was sharing with his six-year-old brother, Joe. There were two sets of bunk beds in the room — one on either side of the window — in case he and Joe brought friends to stay for the weekend.

His mom had spent hours decorating the room in a tropical island theme. He had told her he didn't care what it looked like. After all, he would be spending most of his time on the beach — not in his room. But, he had to admit, she had done a great job. He loved the palm trees that were painted on the walls and he couldn't help but smile when he looked at the unusual shell lamp on the bedside table between the bunks. How he loved to collect shells!

"My sand dollar!" he cried. What had happened to it? Hadn't he found an almost perfect sand dollar? He must have dropped it when he saw . . . His heart began to race. He swallowed hard. What had he seen, exactly?

He could hear his mother's high-pitched voice in the family room. Every so often he heard the voice of Mrs. Fownes, who owned the beach house next door and must have stopped in for a visit.

"I hope he's going to be okay," his mom was saying. "He was delirious . . . babbling on about ghosts and Indians for hours when he came round in the hospital — but what worries me is that he's *still* talking about ghosts and Indians!"

"Poor kid!" answered Mrs. Fownes. "He must have had a terrible fall."

Ghosts and Indians. Yes, that was it. It was all coming back now. The ghost on the bridge, and then the boat full of Spaniards brought in by the waves, and then the Indians. It had certainly seemed very real to him. Could it possibly have all been in his imagination?

His mother reappeared. She placed a glass of orange juice on the bedside table, then leaned over him and felt his forehead with the back of her hand. "Alex, how are you feeling, dear?"

"Much better, thanks, Mom." He gave her a beaming smile deliberately.

"Good. You've got someone who desperately wants to see you."

"Juliann?" he asked hopefully. Juliann Fownes was his best 'vacation friend.' If her mom was over here visiting it seemed reasonable to deduce that Juliann had come too.

"She's been here several times in the past two days to check how you're doing."

"Two days?" asked Alex. "I've been in bed two days?"

"Do you feel up to seeing her?" asked his mom, ignoring the question.

"Sure," said Alex, not *really* sure if he was. But so what? Juliann was a load of fun and his mother might leave him alone for a while.

"Just yell if you need me," said his mom, showing her in.

Juliann strode into the room, her long red ponytail swinging from side to side. She kicked off her flats and flopped down on the other bottom bunk. "Alexander Glass, you're a mess!" she said with a giggle, causing her dimples to deepen. "Have you looked in the mirror lately?"

Alex turned slowly over onto his side to face her. He winced with the pain. "Hey, Juliann, you're supposed to be cheering me up, not depressing me more."

"Seriously, dude," she said. "What's up with your hair? It's all spiky—blond bits are sticking up over the top of that huge white bandage. You look like one of those professional tennis players having a bad hair day."

"Thanks a lot," said Alex. He wanted to laugh but his head hurt too much.

"Sorry," said Juliann. "Just trying to make you laugh, but I guess that's a bad thing right now. Ouch! Look at those huge bruises on your arms! How'd you get those?"

"Do you want my story or my mom's?"

"Which is the most interesting?" she said, leaning forward to hear.

"Oh, mine for sure. But you won't believe me."

"You can tell me. . . I'll believe you, I promise. I won't tell anyone, either."

Alex sighed. "Not sure I believe it myself."

Juliann sat up. "My dad said that everyone in Treasure Island is talking about you falling *over* the handrail of the little footbridge."

"So I've heard."

"It's not true, then? I couldn't work out how you could do that, or how you'd be so badly hurt—it's not exactly high, is it? What *were* you doing — walking along the handrail or something?"

"Yeah, right," said Alex. "I'm not *that* stupid."

"So, dude, what were you doing? Tell me!"

"First, shut the door," said Alex.

Juliann's expression changed. She gave him a quizzical look and then crept to the door, slowly turning the handle to close it without making a sound. "Now you're scaring me, Alex Glass. Did someone hurt you or something? Because you know you should tell someone if they did."

Alex shook his head without thinking and regretted it bitterly. He clenched his teeth until the throbbing eased. "No, no, nothing like that."

"Then, what?" she asked, sitting back on the bed.

"Do you believe in ghosts?" he whispered.

She looked at him for a moment with a stunned expression. "I don't know. I've never really thought about it. I guess I do . . . but I've never seen one, or anything."

"I saw one on the beach. I swear!"

"No way! Really?"

"Mom thinks I had sunstroke—but I'm sure I didn't."

"So what happened?"

"I was on my way back to the beach house when there was this bright flash of red light and then a flash of blue. For a minute I couldn't see—I was blinded, I guess. But when I could see again there was this guy standing on the bridge. He was dressed in a metal hat and weird clothing like he was a wealthy person from medieval times."

"Did he have those long lacy cuffs on his shirt and a fancy ruffled neck, like you see in pictures in the history books?" asked Juliann.

"Yeah, exactly like that."

"And those funny baggy knee-length pants too?"

"Sort of. He also had a cutlass which he was waving around. I think the old Spanish conquistadors used them. I saw pictures of those on the internet when I was researching a project for school last year. His face was scary . . . and I *mean* scary. It was as if his eyes had sunk into his head, or something. And then the light . . . the light from the houses behind seemed to pass right through his body!"

"So did he give you the bruises?"

Alex shook his head and regretted it again.

"So what happened, then?" Juliann asked eagerly.

"He circled above me, slashing his cutlass through the air and wailing, really faintly, 'Malhado! Malhado!'"

"What does that mean?"

"I dunno. But he then told me a whole rhyme. Wish I could remember it—but it was something about Malhado."

Juliann's blue eyes widened and her mouth dropped open. Alex thought she looked like one of the fish his dad had caught. Then she looked at him with a questioning expression and laughed.

"Hey, Alex Glass—you got me! Ghosts don't talk and they sure don't do rhymes. They open and close doors, and things like that. You're making this all up.

26

You're just trying to scare me 'cause you're bored lying here, right?"

Alex felt disappointed. He had felt sure that Juliann would believe him. "I swear, Juliann. I saw this ghost on the bridge. It wasn't as if he was talking, exactly. It was kind of like the wind was whispering and wailing to me . . . something about Malhado."

"For real, Alex?"

"For real."

"And you don't know what Malhado is?"

"Not a clue," said Alex. "Man, it's really bugging me. I think I've heard the word before, but I just can't remember where."

"Maybe we can find out."

"You do believe me, then?" he asked.

She looked at him for a minute as if she were trying to decide whether he was serious. Then she shrugged. "I guess I believe you. I don't *not* believe you!"

Alex smiled. "That's good enough for me. Thanks, Juliann."

The door opened and Alex's mom walked in. "So what are you two whispering about?"

"Nothing," said Juliann.

Alex's mom gave her that look that Alex had seen so many times — the look that moms give you when they know you're up to something.

"Just help me, young lady, by keeping him out of trouble for the rest of this vacation!" she begged.

"I will, Mrs. Glass. I promise."

"Okay, that's enough visiting for today, Alex. You've got to rest. Juliann, please come back tomorrow. You seem to have had a good effect on our invalid."

Alex watched Juliann go to the door. She turned around and gave a little wave. "See you tomorrow, Alex," she said with a grin.

Chapter 4

Alex stood at the bunkroom window staring out over Christmas Bay. It looked so pretty at night with the moon shining over the water.

It had been a long, slow, boring day after Juliann went home—there wasn't much on TV, reading gave him a headache, and his mom had taken his cell phone away so that he wouldn't text friends. "Too much concentration required," she had said. His head still hurt, but at least the heavy throbbing had stopped.

Joe was fast asleep, snoring lightly in the other bottom bunk, and his parents had also turned in for the night. Alex couldn't sleep. He was wide awake and his mind just wouldn't switch off. All he could think about was the ghost on the bridge and everything else that he had witnessed on the beach. He could recount just about all the details, from what the Indian chief had been wearing to what Vaca had said to his men. The only thing he still couldn't remember was the rhyme that the ghost had wailed.

There was nothing like the sound of the sea to make him sleepy. So he crept through the family room and quietly opened the door onto the back deck. The air was so fresh and the sea breeze felt so good. He stood there a while, breathing in deeply and watching the waves crash on the shore. It was a wonderful soothing sound.

What were those lights dancing on the water? He stared a little harder between the houses in front. Was that a ship close to shore? No, ship lights weren't like that, and these lights were way too close to land. There were at least four, flashing like the fireflies he frequently saw in the woods at home. They seemed to be dancing above the waves, turning in circles, first one way and then the other.

Intrigued, Alex held on tightly to the handrail and made his way slowly down the steps to the ground. The full moon on a cloudless night gave him plenty of light. Boy, would his mother have a fit if she knew he was out here after his fall!

He walked between the houses to Gulf Beach Drive—or what was left of it after Hurricane Ike. Unlike at the end of Jolly Roger Road, where sand was piling up and the beach was getting wider every year, there wasn't much of a beach here. There was just a thin strip of sand and lots of rocks.

Alex stood on the edge of the road and scoured the horizon. Where were the lights he had seen from the deck? He couldn't find them now. Suddenly the sea became eerily calm. He had never seen it like this before. There wasn't a sea breeze and there wasn't even a wave in sight! It was as still as a lake on a calm day.

He stood for a moment and watched the water rippling up to the rocks in front of his feet. A chill came over him. There was that same dank smell that he remembered from the beach after the ghost had appeared — only this time it seemed ten times worse. He felt as though he knew what was about to happen. A shiver of fear traced down his spine. He swallowed hard, and was about to turn and run when there was a flash of light — white light this time. It blinded him for a moment. Then there was a second bright flash . . . and a third . . . and a fourth!

Terrified, he fell to his knees.

"Malhado! Malhado!" called an eerie voice in the same three-note wail.

Alex's heart was pounding. He didn't have sunstroke now! He looked up slowly, dreading what he would see. Sure enough, hovering inches above the water directly in front of him was the same ghost in the strange metal hat that he had seen before. But this time there were three other haunting figures behind him—and they were all wailing, "Malhado, Malhado!" Each one had sunken eyes and blue lips, as if they were freezing cold.

"P . . . P . . . Please don't hurt me," begged Alex, cowering.

The ghost with the metal hat seemed to be fixated on Alex. And what was that in his arms? Alex stared in horror. Instead of carrying his cutlass, the ghost was now holding the skull of a large animal!

"Who . . . who . . . who are you?" Alex dared to ask.

The ghost thrust the skull toward Alex. It looked like the head of a cow! It was the most revolting thing, with two holes where its eyes had once been, and an elongated nose with two huge nostrils. Alex couldn't stop shaking.

"Malhado!" whispered the ghost. He raised the cow skull above his head and then, as quickly as he'd appeared, he was gone. The three other ghosts had vanished too.

Alex slouched over his knees, sighing with relief. He felt completely drained of energy. Dare he get up? Dare he walk back to the beach house?

His heart beat was just beginning to slow when a hand gripped his shoulder!

"Ahhh!" Alex screamed, whipping his head around.

His father bent over him. He was wearing his pajamas and a robe, and he didn't look very happy. "Alex, what *are* you doing out here? It's midnight! Your mother would have a fit if she knew."

Alex's heart was racing once again. "Dad! You scared me! How did you know I was down here?"

"Your mother went to bed and I decided to read for a while on the deck. Then I saw you down below walking between the beach houses. What possessed you to come down to the sea at this hour?"

Alex shrugged, unsure of how to respond. 'Possessed' was a good choice of word, he thought.

"You've just had a really nasty fall! Were you sleepwalking?" pressed his father.

Alex still didn't know how to answer the question. One thing was certain—his father wouldn't believe him if he told him what he had just witnessed. "Is that *all* you saw?" asked Alex.

"What do you mean, *is that all I saw*? Should I have seen something else?"

"You didn't see some lights on the water, did you... or a bright flash of white light?"

His father pulled him to his feet. "You probably saw lightning in the distance. They said that there might be a thunderstorm or two tonight. Or maybe you're still recovering from that bump on your head. You can often see white flashing lights when you've had a head injury, you know." He draped his arm around Alex's shoulders as they walked back to Island Sapphire.

Alex decided to say nothing more. How could his father not have seen the light or the ghosts—all four of them? They walked back up the steps and through the family room to the bunkroom. Joe was still fast asleep.

"Now, get into bed and stay there, Alex!" whispered his father. "You need your rest. No more wandering about at night!"

"Dad, please don't tell Mom."

His father sighed deeply and shut the bunkroom door.

Alex took one last look out the window before crawling into the bottom bunk. There was no flash of light to see this time—just the twinkling lights of the

Bright Light general store across the Bluewater Highway. It was a pretty sight, for sure.

"Bright is the light of Malhado," Alex found himself saying as he pulled up the sheets and snuggled into the pillow. Now the ghost had him talking in nonsense rhymes too!

Chapter 5

It was only late morning and already another hot day, but at least there was a pleasant sea breeze. Alex lay in the hammock on the back deck, looking up at the brilliant blue sky. Occasionally, a wisp of white cloud would float by.

Today was the first day that he had put on shorts and a T-shirt instead of swimming trunks. He looked sadly down the road towards the beach. Perhaps he'd be able to go swimming tomorrow. Who was he kidding? He'd be lucky if his mom let him go by the end of the week! She still hadn't let him have his cell phone back.

His head was a lot better today and his mom had removed the bandage, but he still hadn't been able to wash his hair because he had to let the scab heal. He felt disgusting with all that sand and salt—not to mention the blood. How he longed for a shower. He was gently swinging back and forth, thinking about what he had seen the night before, when Juliann tapped him on the shoulder.

He shot up in the air and nearly fell off the hammock. "Hey! Do you have to sneak up on me like that? I've had enough scares in the last couple of days to last me a lifetime!"

"I can't help it if you didn't hear me coming up the steps," she replied indignantly. "You're obviously feeling better this morning!"

"Sorry, Juliann," Alex apologized. "I didn't mean to snap at you. I've just had another rough night."

She looked around as if to check that no one else was in ear shot before whispering, "What? You've seen more ghosts?"

Alex nodded. "You don't have to whisper—everyone else has gone to Galveston for lunch. They promised Joe he could go to Moody Gardens and I promised I'd stay at Island Sapphire and not go on the beach."

"So, come on! Spill it! Who did you see this time?"

"Four of them!" said Alex, swinging his legs over the edge of the hammock and lowering himself carefully to the floor. He walked over to the wooden chairs at the other end of the deck and Juliann sat down next to him.

"You saw *four* ghosts? What . . . all together?" she asked.

"Yep—all at one time."

Juliann looked quite nervous. "They appeared in your bedroom?"

Alex shook his head. Thankfully it didn't hurt to do that today. "Oh, no, nothing like that. I couldn't sleep so I went out onto the deck. I was looking at the waves when I saw some lights over the sea. So I went down to Gulf Beach Drive to have a look."

"What time was this?"

"Midnight."

"Midnight?! You're an idiot, Alex!"

"So everyone keeps telling me."

"Go on then," urged Juliann.

"One ghost was the same one I saw before, and you'll never guess what he was holding this time . . ."

"What? Tell me!"

"A cow's head!"

"Eww, yuk! What . . . was it cut off and bleeding?"

Alex laughed. "No, I meant a *skull*—a cow's skull."

"Really? That's weird!"

"What's even more weird is that my dad came down to get me seconds after that happened and he didn't see any of it. He didn't see the bright flashes of light and he certainly didn't see the ghosts."

"Well, that's possible. Don't ghosts appear only to those they want to see them?"

"I dunno. I don't know much about ghosts at all. So you don't think I've just had a bad fall and I'm hallucinating, which is what everyone else thinks."

She paused for a minute. "I know you had a bad fall, but I also think you saw something."

"So what do I do? Why are the ghosts appearing to me and how do I stop them coming?"

"I have no idea. Sorry, Alex, but I don't know much about ghosts either."

"I could try to find out about Malhado. But who could I ask?"

"I know who'll know!" Juliann said, without even a minute of thought.

"Who?"

"Mrs. Zachariah, our realtor—she was your realtor too."

"Oh yeah, I remember her. She's really nice."

"And remember . . . she's really interested in the history of the area. She knows tons of stuff—like the fact that Surfside used to be called Velasco and it was once the capital of Texas. She used to tell us the history when she was driving us round to look for beach houses."

"But how are we going to get down to her office in Surfside Beach? That's a ten-minute drive! There's no way we can walk it. I guess we could call her, but I don't think she'd believe me over the phone."

"No worries—we don't have to do either! She's with my mom right now," said Juliann with a beaming smile. "She comes over to visit all the time."

Alex sighed. "But if we go over to your beach house and talk to her, your mom will hear. Then you know what will happen . . . your mom will tell my mom that I'm seeing ghosts, and then my mom will panic more, and everyone will think I've *really* damaged my brain!"

"We'll just catch her as she's leaving my house. Come on. We'll sit on the picnic bench under your house and wait for her."

Alex took it slowly down the long flight of steps to the ground, gripping the handrail the entire way. Sixteen feet was a long way to fall when you already had a head injury. He wondered why he hadn't worried about that last night when he climbed down the stairs in the dark! "At least it's cool down here," he said as they reached the bottom step.

They sat on the bench, positioned so that they had a clear view of the steps down from Juliann's beach house. Juliann talked about her life in Dallas, and Alex told her about his life not far away in Houston. He felt lucky that his family was close enough to come down to the beach house for weekends when Juliann could only come a few times a year.

After ten minutes Alex was tired of waiting. "I'd never make a detective," he said. "Stakeouts must be the most boring thing. You do realize that Mrs. Zachariah could be talking to your mom for hours."

"I don't think so," said Juliann, jumping up and waving her arms. "Hey, Mrs. Zachariah!" she shouted. "Can we talk to you for a minute, please?"

Suzan Zachariah was a petite woman. Alex knew his mom envied her delicate features and pretty auburn hair. But until now, Alex had never really noticed anything about Mrs. Zachariah except that her skin was bronzed from living by the Gulf. He thought how wonderful it must be to have a job where you were out and about in the sea breeze, driving people past the beautiful beaches all day long.

He remembered how friendly and helpful she'd been when they were looking for land to build their beach house. Yes, Juliann was right—she was a good bet for information. He also felt that she was the sort of person who would hear him out and not laugh in his face when he mentioned ghosts.

"Hello, Juliann, and hello, Alex," she called as she headed from the foot of the steps in their direction. "I've told you both, you can call me Suzan. It's quite okay, really. Mrs. Zachariah sounds so formal, don't you think?"

"Yes, ma'am," said Alex.

"Okay, Mrs. . . ." Juliann put her hand over her mouth and giggled. "I mean . . . Suzan."

Suzan laughed. "Okay. Ma'am or Suzan—either will do just fine. So, young man, I've just been hearing all about your experience on the beach."

"Yeah, I'm the talk of Treasure Island—but you don't know the half of it," Alex groaned as she sat down opposite him at the picnic table. "You've only heard the adult version!"

"So, tell me the kid version, then," she said, seeming genuinely interested. She removed her cell phone from her bag and laid it carefully on the picnic table. "Just a word of warning before we begin—if my cell phone rings I'm afraid I'll have to take the call. I'm about to close a deal on a house."

42

"That's okay," said Juliann. "We understand you've got work to do."

"So, Alex . . . the kid version then . . .," she said.

"You promise you won't laugh when I tell you?" said Alex, wondering how an adult might react. "It's kind of hard to believe."

She smiled and touched his hand gently. "I promise."

"Okay . . . here goes . . ." Alex took a deep breath. "I've been seeing ghosts."

He waited for her to laugh, but she didn't. She looked him straight in the eye and said, "Go on — tell me everything."

"Do you believe in ghosts, then?" Alex asked.

She pursed her lips together and thought for a minute. "I'll be honest, Alex, I have never had an experience with a ghost, and I don't really know where I stand on the subject. However, I'm always open to the idea that there might be ghosts. Many people believe that the pirate Jean Lafitte haunts Galveston's Trinity Bay, and that Galveston is the most haunted city in Texas and one of the most haunted cities in the U.S.!"

"Really? Galveston?" said Alex. "I never knew that."

"And many people have seen a female ghost wandering at night through the upper room of The Pirate's Alley Café in Surfside Beach," added Suzan.

"Then Alex could *really* have seen a ghost," said Juliann.

Suzan nodded. "I'm sure that some of the local ghost hunters would love to talk to you. In fact, you can actually take a Galveston ghost tour."

"Cool!" said Juliann.

Alex felt so relieved that Suzan was taking him seriously that he just let it all out, hardly stopping to breathe. "I was leaving the beach to come back for dinner when I saw this man on the bridge wearing one of those funny metal hats — like the Spanish conquistadors used to wear — and he was waving a cutlass and wailing at me. . .something about 'Malhado.' Then I saw him a second time last night, and he had three other ghosts with him, and he was holding the skull of a cow! And there was this bright —"

"Whoa!" Suzan interrupted. "Slow down! Slow down! Let me take that all in. Malhado, you said? Carrying the skull of a cow? That's very interesting."

"It is?" Juliann asked. "Do you know what it all means?"

"Have either of you heard of a man called Cabeza de Vaca?"

"I've heard the name before," said Alex.

Juliann scowled. "That was fourth grade history, wasn't it?"

"But I've heard it somewhere else too," said Alex, racking his brains. Why did the name Vaca sound so familiar?

"Cabeza de Vaca was indeed a Spanish conquistador," Suzan continued. "He landed on San Luis Island in 1528. This lovely little neighborhood of Treasure Island has been built where San Luis Island once was."

Alex leapt up. "Treasure Island...our neighborhood ...right here where we're sitting...was once San Luis Island?"

"Sure," said Suzan. "That's why the area is now called San Luis Pass. At one time there was even a bustling city of San Luis — long after Cabeza de Vaca was here, of course. By 1900, because of hurricanes and silt filling up the passes, the city had disappeared and San Luis Island had become part of Follett's Island."

Alex was so excited he could hardly contain himself. "I knew I had heard the name before! Cabeza de Vaca didn't by any chance land here by mistake with a boat that had been wrecked by storms and a crew that was half dead?"

Suzan looked at him with astonishment. "In fact, yes. A lot of his men died from lack of water and food, and a hurricane blew them in this direction. They were lucky to get here at all. How did you know that?"

"Because that's what I saw!" said Alex, almost bursting with excitement.

"Saw? This I gotta hear," said Juliann, rolling her eyes. "Now you saw *tons* of ghosts?"

"Honestly, Juliann," said Alex. "It's a long story, but I saw Cabeza de Vaca's ship smashed by the waves against the shore, and then his men were crawling out of the boat and up the beach. They were all speaking Spanish too, and I heard one of them call him Vaca. It was like I was there . . . with all of them . . . but they couldn't see me. It was like *I* was the ghost watching *them*."

"You didn't tell me any of that before," said Juliann.

"Hey, it was hard enough telling you about seeing one ghost. So, do you know what Malhado means, ma'am?"

"Malhado is the name that Cabeza de Vaca gave to the Island of San Luis. Malhado means the Island of Bad Luck. He was stuck here on the island for over four years and spent another four years wandering around Texas. The cow skull you saw also ties in to the story. Cabeza de Vaca means head of a cow."

"Right!" shouted Alex. "Vaca is a cow. I know a little Spanish. I should have thought about that. I'll bet that he was the ghost that I saw both times. Do you think he was trying to tell me who he was by showing me the cow skull?"

"This is getting too creepy for me," said Juliann, visibly shuddering.

"I must admit," said Suzan, "the whole thing is quite strange. I have to ask you this, Alex: Are you sure you didn't just remember the details from your fourth grade history lessons?"

"I really don't think so, ma'am," said Alex. "We only learned a bit about Cabeza de Vaca in class. There's surely no way I could have remembered it all from fourth grade."

Juliann looked glum. "I don't know how we can find out more—we can't do any research on Cabeza de Vaca, because we don't have a computer with us. My mom always says it's family time when we come to Treasure Island."

"And my dad won't bring his laptop here so that he *can't* do any work and he *has* to take a vacation!" said Alex with a sigh.

"Sensible," said Suzan. "They're both very sensible. Everyone needs a complete break from time to time." She stood up and eased herself out from behind the picnic bench. "Well, Alex, you really have piqued my interest. I'll tell you what . . ." she said, looking at her watch. "I have an appointment right now, but I'll go on the internet tonight and see what I can find out. I'll drop by tomorrow and ask your mom if I can take you and Juliann down to our little history museum in Surfside. In fact, we could even go to the Brazoria County Historical Museum in Angleton, if you really want a lot of information about San Luis Island."

"Sure," said Alex eagerly. "That would be great."

Juliann gave her a hug. "Thanks so much, Suzan. You're the best."

"Yeah, thank you, ma'am," added Alex. "It means a lot that you don't think I'm just seeing things because of the fall I had."

Suzan patted him on the shoulder and laughed. "Hey, I'll reserve judgment for now. But, as I said, there have been reports of ghosts on Galveston Island, so why not here in Treasure Island too? Besides, I'm always open to investigating anything—especially if it has an historical connection."

"I'll see if I can remember the rhyme tonight," said Alex.

"Rhyme?" Suzan questioned, and then looked at her watch again. "Sorry, you'll have to save it for tomorrow."

Alex watched her drive off in her silver car. He felt calmer than he had in a couple of days. At least someone believed him!

Chapter 6

Juliann said she had to go home for lunch, so Alex said goodbye and looked at his watch. It was only one o'clock. His parents would be at least another three or four hours in Galveston, and Juliann was going fishing with her family for the afternoon. He had to find something to do to occupy himself. But what? After the excitement of the last couple of days everything but ghost hunting now seemed so dull.

Reluctantly he climbed the steps back up to Island Sapphire. He stood on the front deck, gazing longingly down Buccaneer Parkway at the beach. The white sand glistened in the sunlight. It seemed to be calling to him. He had promised his mom that he wouldn't go *on* the beach while they were out . . . but she hadn't said that he couldn't walk down the road *to* it, had she?

Alex grabbed his Texans cap from the kitchen counter, locked up the beach house and ambled down Buccaneer Parkway. He felt so much better than he had even a couple of hours before. His head wasn't pounding and his spirits were uplifted after talking with Suzan. He slowed as he got to the end of the street and cut through to Jolly Roger Road.

Ah! There was the little wooden bridge, and beyond, the endless beach. It was so inviting . . . begging him to walk on its sugary sand. Just smelling the sea was enough to make him want to put his foot on the bridge. He felt so sad that he couldn't go any farther. The tide had just turned, and he could just imagine the shells that would be there for collecting . . . but not by him. He felt sick that he was missing out.

The wind whipped up. Alex put his hand on top of his cap to prevent it from blowing away. The sand that had collected in small dunes at the foot of the bridge suddenly began to spiral at his feet. It was like watching several small tornados forming around him. He stood there, completely spellbound by the whirling sand. Faster and faster, higher and higher, the sand circled before his eyes. How strange it was.

Suddenly the sand blew hard at him. The grains stung his cheeks and hurt his eyes. He let go of his cap to protect his face with his hands, but the sand seemed to get everywhere, even up his nostrils. What was happening?

"Ahhh!" shouted Alex. He turned in circles trying to escape the sand, but it was all around him, hitting every part of his exposed skin. Then, just as quickly as it had started, the breeze died and the sand dropped to the ground and settled.

Alex stood there for what seemed an age, shaking uncontrollably. He hardly dared to move or uncover his eyes. Had it really stopped?

Finally he had the nerve to take his hands from his face. The day was as it had been before—bright sunlight with hardly a breeze—and the houses were still all around him. Thank goodness he was okay!

"Gross!" Alex spat out the sand from his mouth.

He picked his cap off the ground and shook it. His shoes were covered in sand too. But what was that in front of his feet? He stared at the ground in disbelief. There, at the foot of the bridge, were some words traced in the sand! It was as if someone had taken a stick and scrawled in old-fashioned cursive writing. Amazingly, the sand hadn't fallen back to fill in the grooves cut out by the letters. The words were clear.

"Bright is the Lite of Malhado. Alvar Nuñez Cabeza de Vaca," Alex read.

His heart quickened. He stepped back, expecting to see the ghost once again, but there was no flash of light, no dank smell and no sign of him.

"Cabeza de Vaca," he called, his voice quaking. "Are you there?"

Alex waited anxiously, frightened that he might actually appear. He turned in circles, but there was no sign of the ghost. In fact, now he felt quite disappointed that Cabeza de Vaca hadn't appeared for a third time! How could he feel like that when the ghost had scared him so much? Was he crazy to *want* to see him?

Alex stood staring at the curly lettering for a few more minutes, trying to work out what the message meant. Perhaps the ghost was waiting for him on the beach? He stepped over the writing and stood at the foot of the bridge. He desperately wanted to cross over the bridge and onto the sand, but he had promised his mom. Surely he could stand in the middle of the bridge—that wasn't going *on* the beach exactly, was it?

He walked boldly to the middle of the bridge, almost expecting it to shake. He gripped the handrail and looked down the beach, but today there was no ghost sighting. Anyway, didn't ghosts only appear after dusk?

Still unnerved from his experience, he sat down in the center of the bridge. He wouldn't be lying to his mom. He wasn't on the beach — just on the bridge — and she didn't say he couldn't go there.

He visualized the boat that he had seen come crashing out of the waves and onto the sand in his dream. His dream? Is that what it was? Had he collapsed with sunstroke or fallen off the bridge somehow after he had seen the ghost?

"How could I have fallen off this little thing?" he asked himself, touching the wood he was sitting on. Juliann had been right. He could have been injured only if he'd been walking along the handrail. "And I don't do such dumb things!" he growled.

Of one thing he was sure, and no one would be able to convince him otherwise: he *had* seen the ghost of Cabeza de Vaca . . . twice! And now the ghost was leaving him messages too!

"Bright is the Lite of Malhado," Alex muttered. Isn't that what he had said to himself when he got into bed the other night, when he was joking about making up rhymes like the ghost? How weird that the ghost should write the same thing in the sand! Did the sentence really mean something?

He sighed. Thanks to his mom, he didn't have his cell phone to take a picture of the writing as proof—and there was no one on the beach to show, either. He wondered if even Juliann and Suzan would believe him.

He tried to recall the rhyme that the ghost had wailed the first time. "Alvar Nuñez Cabeza de Vaca," said Alex out loud. "What are you trying to tell me?" Thank goodness there was no one on the beach right now—if anyone could hear him talking to himself, it would only add to the neighborhood gossip that he had lost his mind when he fell off the bridge!

Since talking to Suzan, some of the rhyme was now quite clear. Malhado definitely referred to San Luis Island, which really was where he was sitting right now. He remembered something in the rhyme about a heavy loss of flesh and treasure, but he couldn't remember the exact words.

Suzan had said that a lot of Cabeza de Vaca's men had died at sea, so that could be the flesh part. But what about the treasure? Did Cabeza de Vaca lose treasure at sea as well as his men?

He thought hard for a minute and then the rhyme came to him. "'I cannot rest! I cannot go! While 'tis buried on Malhado!'" He jumped up in his excitement. That was it! Those were the last two lines of the rhyme.

Cabeza de Vaca didn't lose the treasure at sea at all. He buried it on Malhado! And that meant he buried it in Treasure Island!

"I'll find your treasure, Cabeza de Vaca . . . I promise," he yelled into the sea breeze. "'Tis buried on Malhado!" he said again, laughing. Unbelievable! He hadn't for once imagined that his little neighborhood of Treasure Island might really have buried treasure. Excitement consumed him. What if he could find Cabeza de Vaca's treasure?

Alex turned around on the bridge and focused on the piece of land that jutted out into the sea just past the beach. He thought back to how he had followed Cabeza de Vaca round a point and along the beach. Could that be the same place? Nearly 500 years had passed since Cabeza de Vaca had first landed on San Luis Island. Would the coastline have changed much in all those centuries?

Alex walked off the bridge and decided to take another look at the writing in the sand. But where was it? Small mounds of sand lay heaped at the foot of the bridge where the writing had been. There was no trace of the words at all, and he had no proof of what he had seen to show anyone. He could just hear his mother say, "Alex Glass, what a vivid imagination you have!"

He walked away from the bridge and headed round the point to Gulf Beach Drive, once again feeling crestfallen. What a roller coaster ride he was on—one minute he was terrified, and the next he was either consumed with excitement or totally miserable.

He arrived at the house that was now built on the point. It had been badly battered by Hurricane Ike, but the owners were rebuilding. All around the point and very close to the base of the house were large rocks and boulders. Rocks? He had trudged after Cabeza de Vaca round the point and across a beach littered with oyster shells. He hadn't seen any rocks! Had it always been a rocky coastline here? The answer was important.

Alex's heart was racing. He walked along Gulf Beach Drive, looking out to sea. There were huge boulders piled up all along the edge of the road.

One of the homeowners on Gulf Beach Drive was getting out of his car.

"Excuse me, sir. Can I ask you a question?"

"Sure. How can I help?"

"I'm Alex Glass. My family has a beach house just behind you on Buccaneer. I'm interested in the history of Treasure Island."

"Nice to meet you, Alex. I'm Jack Evans. What do you want to know? I don't know much of the history, I'm afraid."

"Well, I guess it's really the geography of Treasure Island that I have a question about. Have these boulders along the edge of the road been here a long time?"

Jack Evans laughed. "I can answer that one easily. These boulders were put here by FEMA only two years ago, just after Ike."

"FEMA?" questioned Alex.

"FEMA stands for Federal Emergency Management Agency. They are the government agency that responds after disasters, helping communities get their lives back together. "

"Oh," said Alex. "I think I've heard about them on the news."

"Before Ike we had a beautiful beach on this side of the point. The beach has eroded so much just in the last few years that FEMA and our community association are doing everything they can to save the road, because that's what'll go next. See those wooden pilings?" He pointed out to sea to some pieces of wood that protruded above the waves. "There was a house there two years ago!"

Alex stared at him. "No kidding! For real?"

"In fact, we've lost several others along this road too."

"So, hundreds of years ago . . ."

Jack Evans smiled and pointed out to sea once again. "Hundreds of years ago the beach was way out there!"

"Oh," said Alex. "We've studied erosion in Geography, but I didn't realize how bad it was."

"My wife and I have been here twenty-three years. The beach on this side of Treasure Island was quite wide when we built this house. I guess it was wider than the beach off Jolly Roger Road. Now look at us! We're virtually in the water—but at least we have a great sea view," he added with a chuckle.

"Thanks for your time, Mr. Evans."

"Anytime, Alex. Have a good one."

Alex headed back to Island Sapphire feeling utterly dejected. He had followed Cabeza de Vaca round the point. He had watched him hide something in the sand. What was it? Where was it now? Alex sighed. If Cabeza de Vaca had hidden something along this part of Treasure Island's coast, then it was long gone—swallowed up by the sea hundreds of years ago. His treasure hunting hadn't lasted long, had it?

The dream of finding treasure would stay a dream. But then, why did the ghost of Cabeza de Vaca keep appearing to him? And why would he mention buried treasure if there wasn't any to be found? There had to be a reason.

Chapter 7

Alex saw Suzan's car pull up outside Island Sapphire. "I thought you weren't coming until tomorrow!" he shouted from the deck.

She looked at her cell phone as she approached the house, and waved a manila folder at him. "My appointment got cancelled and so I spent a couple of hours doing some research on your ghost instead."

"You did?" said Alex excitedly. "Thanks!"

"I thought you might be eager to see what I found... or I can come back tomorrow, if you're busy," she added with a smirk.

Alex nearly fell down the steps in an effort to stop her from leaving. "Oh, no, ma'am—don't do that—I'm really pleased you're here. I can't think of anything but Cabeza de Vaca right now. It's driving me crazy. It's like one of those songs you can't get out of your head. I keep going over and over everything."

"And you're still convinced you saw a ghost?"

"Yes, ma'am! Even more after today's experience!"

"Today's experience?" she said, her jaw dropping. "Never mind," she waved her hand in the air. "Save it for now. Let's concentrate on what I've found out and you can tell me that story afterward."

She sat down at the picnic bench under Island Sapphire. "Okay, then. First, everything I said about Cabeza de Vaca this morning is correct. What's more interesting is that everything you told me that you saw on the beach is also correct. Cabeza de Vaca landed on San Luis Island in 1528 — "

"November 6, 1528, right?" Alex interrupted.

Suzan looked astonished. "Yes, that's right. Did you remember that from fourth grade?"

Alex shook his head. "When I was watching Cabeza de Vaca on the beach I heard him say to his men in Spanish, 'It is the sixth of the month of November.' They couldn't hear me or see me, but I was so confused I shouted back 'No, it's June 16th.'"

"Okay, so the date connects too. Let's look at some of the other details. You told me that the second time the ghost appeared he had three other ghosts with him."

"Yes, ma'am."

"Cabeza de Vaca survived for four years on San Luis Island as a slave to the Indians. Apart from Cabeza de Vaca, there were only three other survivors from the original royal expedition."

"So those could have been the three other ghosts I saw."

Suzan nodded. "Could be. Now, before I go any further, tell me about the rhyme—the one you mentioned this morning."

"Well, I didn't exactly see the ghost's mouth move or anything like that, but I did hear the ghost say something about a loss of flesh and treasure, and that he couldn't go while it was buried on Malhado."

Suzan raised her eyebrows. "So you think Cabeza de Vaca buried his treasure all those years ago on San Luis Island?"

"That's what I'm thinking. And you said that our neighborhood, Treasure Island, is where San Luis Island used to be, right?"

Suzan nodded. "Correct."

"Is there anything in the history books about Cabeza de Vaca's treasure? I mean, if the pirate Jean Lafitte is still looking for his treasure in Galveston, why wouldn't

Cabeza de Vaca be looking for his treasure on San Luis Island?"

Suzan pursed her lips and thought for a moment. "I'm not sure about that, Alex. Cabeza de Vaca wrote his own account of his time here on San Luis Island, which has been translated into English since. You can actually read it online. As far as I know, it doesn't mention anything about burying treasure."

"But he wouldn't mention it, would he? I mean, he wouldn't *want* anyone to know about it—especially if he thought he'd be able to come back and get it."

"That could be true, but it seems he and his men lost just about everything, either in Florida, or at sea before they landed here. According to his memoirs they traded bells and beads with the Indians, not gold or treasure."

"But I saw him give the Indian chief—"

"Indian chief?" Suzan cut in. "You didn't tell me you saw Indian spirits too! Juliann's mom said that you were talking about Indians when you were in the hospital."

"Just after I saw the ghost the first time, it was like I was there on the beach. I can't explain it, ma'am. But I saw Cabeza de Vaca give the Indian chief a necklace of dark blue stones. You should see how the gems caught the sunlight. They sparkled like nothing I've ever seen before. I know a lot about shells, rocks and gems, and I swear it was a sapphire necklace he gave to the chief. No *way* was it shells or beads!"

"Well, I don't know what to say, Alex. I don't *not* believe you—it's just hard to wrap my mind around something like this."

"I know," said Alex. He let out a deep breath. "It's even harder for me, because I really think it happened—but I daren't tell anyone else because of the accident. Everyone thinks I was hallucinating."

"That does sort of tie in to my research too."

"How do you mean?"

"Well, because some scientists believe that how we perceive a ghost might be related to hallucinations, imagination, our dreams and our emotions. We all have hallucinations when we dream, and it is known that some diseases and medicines can make people hallucinate. After your trip to the hospital it would be natural for most people to connect your ghost experience to your fall."

"But that doesn't explain how several people can see a ghost at the same time," said Alex. "I know I've heard stories about ghosts being seen by two people at once."

"That's quite true. I've heard those stories too. So let me read to you what I found out."

"Sure," said Alex, hanging on her every word.

"You have to understand that there is so much information about ghosts, with lots of differing opinions on the subject. So I only had time to take notes on a little of it."

"Sure," said Alex again, desperate for her to begin.

She opened the folder and began reading from her notes. "Now remember . . . this is just what I got from my research. I'm not saying it is true or that I believe it. You have to weigh everything and make your own decision."

"Okay," said Alex. "Understood."

"It seems that most ghosts are spirits, which is the nonphysical part of us."

"You mean that a ghost is the soul of someone who is dead," said Alex.

Suzan nodded. "Exactly. A ghost can appear to us as a light, a figure or a noise, or by making objects move."

"A light?" questioned Alex.

"Does that mean something to you?" asked Suzan.

"Maybe. I saw flashing lights before I saw Cabeza de Vaca . . . both times. Blue and red flashing ones the first time, and white the second."

"Have you considered that those could be connected to your head injury and not to the ghosts appearing?" asked Suzan. "You do know that your father called an ambulance when he found you, right? The blue and red flashing lights could have been that."

Alex nodded. "Yeah, I had thought about that."

"And often people see white flashing lights after a head injury or if they suffer from migraines."

"So my dad said," said Alex.

"If you keep seeing flashing lights you should get yourself checked out."

"Don't worry, I have to go back to the hospital for a checkup at the end of the week," said Alex.

"Good. Then I won't worry. Well, let me tell you what else I found out." She continued to read from her notes. "Ghosts often appear in our dreams, and it is believed that a lot of people who communicate with ghosts do so in their sleep. But, when we are awake, places like old buildings, prisons, factories, and even towns out in the countryside where very emotional things have happened, can create an atmosphere where ghosts can be seen more easily."

"So, like the beach on Malhado for Cabeza de Vaca," said Alex, desperate to make a connection.

"Could be," said Suzan. "This next bit of information I found very interesting . . . ghosts can be attracted by the emotional energy we each give off."

"So, you mean that because I love Treasure Island so much, and love finding shells and things on the beach, Cabeza de Vaca appears to me because he thinks I'm looking for his lost treasure?"

Suzan shrugged. "I'm not sure about that, Alex, but you never know. I really wish I knew more about ghosts. But like you, I'm just trying to make a bit of sense from what has happened to you."

"Did you find out anything else?"

Suzan nodded. She turned the paper over and continued. "Ghosts are not physical at all and so they cannot speak as they don't have vocal chords."

"But I heard him! I swear I did!" said Alex, feeling suddenly defensive.

"Well, hold on a minute," said Suzan. "It seems that a lot of people believe that we can see and hear ghosts. But the most common belief is that we see and hear ghosts telepathically. In other words, you hear the ghost in your mind and what you see is also in your mind, like being in two places at one time."

Alex sat up straight again. "So, like I'm on the beach in our time, but I'm feeling like I'm back in the past 500 years ago with Cabeza de Vaca."

Suzan smiled. "I guess so. Now, you were going to tell me what happened today."

"Can I ask you a question first?"

"Sure. Ask away."

"Was Cabeza de Vaca's full name Alvar Nuñez Cabeza de Vaca?"

Suzan looked at him with a quizzical expression. "It was. Now I suppose you're going to tell me that he told you that today!"

"He didn't actually *tell* me . . . he wrote a message telling me."

Suzan's eyes were wide. "Show me!"

Alex bit his lip. He knew she would say that! Why couldn't he just have got some proof to show someone? "I can't show you because Cabeza de Vaca wrote it in the sand and now all the writing has been blown over by more sand."

"Oh," she said faintly.

"I can tell from your voice that you don't believe me. But he did, I swear. He also wrote 'Bright is the Lite of Malhado.' Light was spelled wrong."

"What do you mean by *spelled wrong*?"

"It was spelled l-i-t-e instead of the normal way."

"So what do you make of that?" Suzan asked.

"I have no clue. I think that Cabeza de Vaca saw me spending all that time looking for shells on the beach and he thinks that I might be able to find his treasure, especially after everything you've said today about ghosts having emotional connections with people, and haunting places where emotional things have happened. I love it here. Maybe he knows that."

"But Cabeza de Vaca *hated* San Luis Island!" said Suzan. "That's why he called it Malhado, Bad Luck Island."

"Maybe he learned to love it after living here for so long! How long did you say he was on Malhado?"

"At least four years," said Suzan.

"Well then, it's possible, isn't it? Maybe he hated being a slave to the Indians but perhaps he loved the island itself . . . like I do. I know you just think I'm trying to find reasons for everything that has happened to me, and I guess I am. It's all very confusing, but a lot of it does seem to fit together, don't you think?" said Alex.

Suzan sighed. "I don't know what to think anymore. I don't know if I've helped you or made things worse."

"Oh, you *have* helped me! I really believe I've seen the ghost of Cabeza de Vaca and that he's trying to talk to me."

"That's what worries me," said Suzan with a laugh. "Do you still want to do more research on San Luis Island?"

"Definitely!" said Alex.

"Then we'll go to the museums tomorrow. Your mom has my cell number. Just call me in the morning and I'll come and get you and Juliann."

"Thanks, ma'am . . . Suzan. I really do appreciate you trying to help me."

"No problem, Alex. Besides, I love a good mystery and *I'm* learning things too!"

Chapter 8

Alex grabbed his towel from the bathroom rail—he finally felt human again. His mom had returned his cell phone and she had let him take a shower. What more could he want? He ran his hands through his wet hair, delighting in the squeakiness, but being careful not to touch the sore patch at the back of his head. Clean was good, he decided.

His phone beeped loudly as he walked into his bedroom.

"Get your phone, Alex!" his mom shouted from the kitchen.

"Okay!" Alex yelled back, diving on the bed to reach it. It was a text from Juliann. He texted back. "Juliann wants me to go over there," he yelled again. "Can I?"

"Alex, stop shouting from room to room! Come and talk to me if you want a response."

Alex threw on some clothes and walked into the kitchen. His mom was loading the dishwasher.

"I can see we're back to normal," she said. "It's 8:00 p.m. Be back here by 10 o'clock—and don't get up to any trouble. You stay with Juliann. I don't want your father to have to go out looking for you in the dark again!"

"I promise," Alex groaned. He could see that he was never going to live down this whole incident. It was the sort of thing his mom would be telling everyone at every family party for years to come.

Juliann met him at the bottom of the steps. "Dude, your mom let you out! Amazing!"

Alex sighed, "Not without a lecture first."

"She'll be watching you like a hawk for weeks."

Alex moaned. "Don't I know it! Man, I hope she gets over it quick!"

"So, are you ready to go ghost-busting?" she asked with a giggle.

"Hey, this is serious stuff," said Alex, feeling a little annoyed at her flippant attitude. "I told you what Suzan found out, and I told you what happened to me this afternoon. It's no joke, you know!"

"I know, I'm sorry," she responded in a more serious tone. "But I thought that if I could see the ghost too, then perhaps everyone would believe you. See . . . I even came prepared." She waved a flashlight at him.

"If you're really sure you want to do this . . . and you're not going to get scared or anything . . ."

"Who, me? When do I get scared? I must be the only girl for miles around that loves spiders—and I'm not afraid of snakes, skinning fish or petting iguanas!"

Alex pulled a face at her. "Okay, but I gotta be back by 10 o'clock."

"That's almost two hours to find a ghost!" she said excitedly. "So where do we start?"

"The footbridge," said Alex, grabbing her shoulders and turning her down Buccaneer Parkway.

It was a beautiful clear evening and the sun was just going down. The air was fresh and a gentle breeze made the palm trees rustle.

"Nervous yet?" asked Alex.

"Nah," said Juliann. "I've always wanted to see a ghost."

"Right." He wondered how she might react if Cabeza de Vaca *did* appear—especially if he were carrying that ghastly cow's skull. Petting lizards was one thing; talking to a ghost was another! He decided that she really didn't get it.

They stood together in the center of the bridge, looking first over Christmas Bay at the sun slowly dipping below the horizon, and then out to sea at the waves crashing on the shore in the low light. It was the most wonderful place to be. For a minute Alex forgot about ghosts. He just stood there and enjoyed his surroundings. He wished the summer would last forever so that he never had to leave this magical place.

"Do we have to be silent for the ghost to come?" Juliann whispered.

"Dunno," said Alex. "Might be the best thing."

"We could try calling him, like you said you did this afternoon."

"But he didn't come when I did that."

Juliann sighed. "Well, I guess we just wait, then."

Twenty minutes passed. Neither of them said a word in that time and it was nearly dark. There was no sign of any ghost.

Thirty minutes passed. Juliann sat down on the bridge but Alex decided to stay standing. He gripped the handrail . . . just in case. Still they hadn't said a word, and still there was no sign of any ghost.

Forty minutes passed. Alex decided to sit down too. Juliann looked like she'd fallen asleep and Alex was trying hard to stay awake. Still no sign of Cabeza de Vaca.

"Okay, that's it!" said Alex when forty-five minutes had passed. "I can't do this anymore tonight. I guess he's not going to appear."

Juliann yawned and stretched her arms above her head. "I guess he's not shown himself because I'm here too," she said sadly.

Alex shrugged. "Dunno . . . anyway, it's nearly nine o'clock. Do you want to walk over the road to the Bright Light and get some candy from Debbie?"

"Sure," she replied. "We've still got an hour before you have to be back at the beach house."

They walked back along Buccaneer, passing both of their houses on the way, and turned onto Palm Avenue in the direction of the main road.

It was quite dark as they left the houses behind and approached the entrance to the neighborhood. The lights of the Bright Light general store shone across Bluewater Highway, lighting up the tower at the entrance toTreasure Island.

"I've always wondered what this funny brown tower is," said Juliann as they approached.

Alex looked up. "Someone said it's the housing for the telephones in Treasure Island."

"Really? It's like a little wooden house on stilts. And what's with the metal cage at the back and the weird looking triangular tower at the front?"

"The triangular bit's got a spiral staircase in it. It goes up to the balcony," said Alex. "Look—you can just see the white handrail at the top."

"It's pretty spooky, if you ask me—especially at night. I wouldn't want to go up there—even in the day time, and even if it were only to check telephone connections. See, it's got two doors and that funny little balcony—"

Suddenly Juliann grabbed Alex's arm. He could feel her fingernails digging into his skin. "Juliann! What are you—?"

"Shhh! Dude, do you see that?" she asked. "Look! Look up!"

He wanted to unpeel her fingers from his arm but he found himself looking up instead.

"There's someone up there," she whispered. "Do you see?"

He stared up at the tower. It was hard to see in the dark, but yes, there was definitely someone standing on the balcony looking down at them. "You're right," said Alex. "I see someone."

"Is it the ghost of Cabeza de Vaca?" Her voice quaked.

Alex could feel her trembling, or was it his own legs shaking? "No, it doesn't look like Cabeza de Vaca. It's a woman, I think."

"What's she doing up there?"

"How should I know?" whispered Alex.

"She doesn't look like someone who works for the telephone company. Do you think it's someone from the neighborhood?"

Alex couldn't take his eyes away. Yes, it was definitely a woman . . . an older woman wearing a long, dark dress and a funny hat.

"She's doing something with her hands," said Juliann. "I think she's waving to us."

"*No,* she's telling us to come up. Shine the light up there," Alex ordered.

Juliann concentrated the beam on the woman. "Ahhh!" she screamed and dropped the flashlight. "Did you see? Did you see, Alex? The light went right through her!"

Alex prised Juliann's left hand off his arm and picked up the flashlight. Quickly he shone it back up at the deck. "Where is she?" He scanned the beam across the balcony and then down the sides of the tower. "I don't see her, do you?"

"Maybe she came down," said Juliann, her voice trembling.

Alex shone the flashlight everywhere, back and forth around the tower, up and down the tower, and back up at the balcony. "Man . . . she's disappeared!"

"But she can't have. We would have seen her come down the tower . . . or walk away!"

He looked at Juliann. "Not if she's a ghost," he said.

Juliann was silent.

"You did say you could see right through her!" Alex added.

"I did . . . I could," Juliann stammered.

"So now do you believe me?" asked Alex.

Juliann nodded. "I think we should go home," she said quietly.

Chapter 9

Alex tossed and turned. He plumped his pillow, rolled onto his stomach, rolled back again, and finally lay there staring up at the bunk above. He sighed heavily. He didn't want to sleep. How could he even think about sleeping after what had happened tonight? He wanted to be outside looking for that woman!

When Juliann had suggested that they go ghost hunting, he never *really* thought they would see a ghost together. Now she was probably feeling the same fear and confusion he had felt the day before. He could tell she had been shaken by the experience—she hadn't said a word all the way back to the beach house.

And what exactly *had* they experienced? They had both seen a woman up on the balcony of the telephone exchange—there was no question about that. The beam of light had shone right through her body—just like he had witnessed with Cabeza de Vaca. And then the woman had disappeared . . . vanished into thin air without a trace. She had to have been a ghost. What other explanation could there be? Juliann thought she had been waving at them, but he was positive that she had been beckoning. There was a big difference between the two. Had the ghost wanted them to come up the tower?

Enough with trying to sleep! Quietly, he threw back his covers, swung his legs to the floor and checked to make sure that Joe was fast asleep. Good—he was snoring as usual.

Alex tiptoed across the room, pulled his sports shorts over his boxers and slipped his feet into his flip-flops. Slowly he turned the door handle, cringing as the door creaked. Finally, he opened it enough to squeeze through, and crept into the kitchen. The flashlight was still on the kitchen countertop where he had dumped it earlier. It was all he needed. He scooped it up and walked silently out the kitchen door.

Alex stood under one of the tall Mexican fan palms in front of Juliann's house, looking up at her room and enjoying the cool air. Her curtains were drawn and there was no sign of light. He wondered whether she was fast asleep or lying in the dark, still frightened by their ghostly encounter. So why was he stupid enough to go looking for ghosts twice in one night? Wasn't he just asking for trouble? Just because Cabeza de Vaca had never harmed him didn't mean that another ghost wouldn't. He gulped. Perhaps he really shouldn't be out here at midnight chasing ghosts!

But now his feet seemed to be leading him down the road. He jogged down Palm Avenue, slowing as he approached the telephone exchange. At first glance it seemed a perfectly normal structure, like the ones he saw all over the barrier islands — just a little eerie in the moonlight. He walked all around the base of the tower, shining the flashlight up and down, and especially at the balcony. There was no sign of any ghost.

Without a second thought he entered the little triangular tower and began to climb the spiral staircase. It wasn't easy with a flashlight in one hand. The stairs were narrow and turned tightly, and he found it difficult to get a foothold, but he clung to the metal handrail and took each step slowly and carefully. What had possessed him to do this?

His heart quickened as he neared the top. Just as he started to haul himself onto the balcony, a dark female figure suddenly appeared directly in front of him, blocking his path!

"Ahhhhh!" Alex screamed, losing his grip on the handrail. The flashlight plummeted to the ground, smashing on the concrete below. He held on tightly with his other hand, looking up at the figure. His legs were shaking so much that he worried he would lose his footing on the narrow staircase. Why had he screamed at the sight of the ghost? Isn't this what he wanted? Hadn't he come in search of ghosts?

He drew in a deep breath. Yes, it was the same woman they had seen earlier. She was clothed from head to foot in a black dress, and wore a black bonnet trimmed with lace and tied with a big bow under her chin. And now he could see her face. Her complexion was ashen white — almost as if she had taken thick white powder and plastered it on her skin. Her eyes were darkly rimmed with deep circles under her eyes. She stepped back from the staircase and beckoned him to follow.

Alex hesitated. Should he do as she was asking or climb down and run home? Somehow his feet left the staircase and, before he knew it, he was standing on the balcony less than five feet away from her.

"Why are you out so late, young man?" she seemed to whisper in his ear — and yet she hadn't moved close to him and her lips hadn't moved, either! Her tone sounded like a reprimand — rather like his mother's voice when he was in trouble.

"Alexander, you should be in bed!"

Alex was stunned. Did she just mention him by name? "W . . . what did you say?"

"Where is Juliann? You were supposed to stay with her!"

And now she knew about Juliann too? How could that be?

She moved toward him. "I expect you've been looking for buried treasure again! You should have been looking after Juliann!"

Alex felt sick. This was just too weird. The woman's face suddenly changed and took on an angry expression. Her complexion seemed even whiter under the moonlight. Her eyes bore right through him. She moved even closer, wagging her finger aggressively. "Alexander, I am so disappointed in you. This is the last time I am going to tell you to stop wasting your time down on the beach. You are responsible for Juliann!"

Alex stepped back to avoid her. His heel went over the edge of the top step of the spiral staircase. He stumbled . . . tried to catch hold of the railing . . . his hands were madly grabbing to hold on. He felt the metal hit his legs . . . graze his shins. He was falling . . . his head hit the railing . . . oh—his head!

Chapter 10

Alex groaned. How his head pounded . . . again!
But at least he could move his legs and arms. It didn't
seem as though he had broken anything. What was he
thinking by climbing those stupid stairs in the dark and
chasing more ghosts! He knew he would be in serious
trouble if he didn't get home and into bed before
someone realized he was gone. How would he explain
the new bruises on his arms and that deep gash on his
leg? What about the stitches in his head? If he'd
reopened the wound his mom would ground him for
years!

Alex staggered to his feet and brushed himself
down. Grass clung to his sports shorts.

"Grass?" he questioned aloud. How did he fall on
grass when there was a concrete pad beneath the tower?

His heart raced as he looked around in the bright sunlight. "*Sun*light? Where's the darkness? Oh no! It's happened again!" he yelled, panic struck. "This *can't* have happened to me again!"

But it had. This place certainly wasn't the Treasure Island that he knew. He was standing on a dirt road in the middle of nowhere. There were no brightly colored houses built sixteen feet off the ground, no tower, no Bluewater Highway and no Bright Light general store. Alex was stunned.

He stood there, a lump in his throat. His mind was buzzing with questions. How could he get home again when he couldn't even *see* his beach house? Was he still in Treasure Island but in a different time period? What should he do? Where should he go?

There was only one road—if you could call it that—and he was standing on it. Maybe he should just follow it . . .

"Walk! Walk, you idiot!" Alex said to himself. "You can't stand here in the heat all day!" For once, his feet seemed reluctant to move, but he forced himself to take a step, even though it hurt to do so. The bruises were bad and he could feel blood trickling down his leg.

Alex hobbled along the dirt track for what seemed an age. His mouth was dry and every bone in his body ached. He was considering sitting down for a rest when he heard a rumbling noise. He looked behind just in time to leap to one side as a wagon pulled by two dark brown horses came roaring past.

"Hey! Watch out!" Alex screamed as he hit the ground. It was as if the driver hadn't seen him! The driver smacked his whip and the horses picked up more speed, disappearing in a cloud of dust. Alex coughed and spluttered. How he longed for some water.

He picked himself up, wincing in pain, and trudged on, feeling even more discouraged. The road seemed to be going nowhere. But then, as he stared into the distance across the waving grass, he yelled in delight, "Houses! I can see houses!" Yes, there were definitely buildings of some kind in the distance, and buildings usually meant people. Surely he could find someone to help him there. He picked up his pace, even though it hurt to do so.

After a few minutes the dirt track turned a corner. Alex rounded the bend and stared in disbelief. "Water!" he shouted joyously. "It's a lake!" He ran down to the edge and hurriedly scooped as much as he could into his mouth. He spat it straight out and wiped his tongue on his sleeve. "Oh, yuk! It's sea water!"

Of course it was sea water . . . he had just been so thirsty that he hadn't noticed the obvious signs—the white sand beach, the shells, the crab holes . . . and, of course, the fresh salty smell of sea air. But where were the waves? There was just a gentle rippling of water against the shore.

Alex thought for a minute. His geography wasn't very good, but he did know that Treasure Island was in San Luis Pass at the tip of Follett's Island, and was surrounded by water. The Gulf of Mexico was on one side and Cold Water Pass on the other. He'd never really looked at what was on the other side of the pass. Could there have been houses that he hadn't noticed before?

Alex heard a noise. He watched as an old-fashioned black buggy rattled round the corner and pulled up close to what appeared to be a small dock. Alex had never seen a buggy except in history books. What was one doing on Follett's Island? It had four huge wheels with spokes. The two front wheels were slightly smaller than those at the rear, and a canopy covered the seat. A short burly man got down from the buggy and then offered his hand to a lady, who carefully climbed down the steps.

They were both dressed in old-fashioned clothing as if they were going to a fancy dress party. The man wore a dark suit with tails, a fancy cravat and a top hat. The lady looked as though she were burning up in a heavy, long, red dress, which puffed out with layers of petticoats. She linked her arm through the man's and twirled her red parasol over her shoulder as they walked onto the dock. They stood still near the edge of the dock for a while and seemed to be waiting . . . but for what?

Alex looked across the water. Was that a ferry he could see on the other side? For the first time he noticed that next to him was a huge wooden post with a pulley attached to it. He watched as the rope moved through the pulley and the ferry came closer and closer.

Alex limped over to the couple and asked, "Excuse me, but is this the line for the ferry?"

The man ignored him and continued to talk to the elegant lady with the fancy parasol. Alex waved his hand directly in front of the man's face. No reaction. He jumped up and down in front of the lady—but she carried on talking, oblivious to his wild behavior.

Alex felt sick. Now he understood why the wagon driver had nearly run him over on the road. Once again he had become the ghost observing everyone else . . . just as he had been on the beach, watching Cabeza de Vaca and his men. How would he get home again?

The little ferry pulled up to the dock. It was just a simple raft with a rail down each side. The two passengers paid for their tickets and climbed aboard. Alex followed behind. Perhaps it was a good thing that no one could see him since he had no money to pay for the ferry ride! He stood at the front of the ferry, eagerly watching the shoreline on the other side as the ferry took them closer and closer.

Within minutes he was able to make out the buildings more clearly. He could count at least a dozen houses facing the water, and there were definitely more houses behind. They were simple wooden structures, with shutters on either side of the small-paned windows, and each house also had a porch across the entire front. Very few houses had been painted.

The ferry slowed and pulled up to the dock. Alex disembarked and stood under a sign post. "Liberty Street one way, and South Street the other," he muttered, wondering which way he should go. Did it even matter?

He began walking down Liberty Street, away from the dock. Some of the homes on this street were more elegant than those facing the water, and looked like little wooden gingerbread houses. The roofs were steeply pitched, and the pointed arches were trimmed with lacy wooden edging. Some had wooden verandas that were elaborately decorated.

He looked from side to side, trying to take in every detail. Several more houses were being built, and the noise of hammering added to the other unfamiliar sounds. Horses were tied up to hitching posts in front of some of the buildings, and he could see a general store, a blacksmith and a hotel.

When he had almost reached the end of Liberty Street he could see the white crests of waves offshore. "The sea!" he said, excited by the sight of something familiar.

He spotted the local newspaper office at the corner of Liberty and Market streets. Alex looked up and read on a board above the window, "*San Luis Advocate.*"

"San Luis?" he questioned. "Am I really in San Luis?"

His heart quickened. He remembered what Suzan had said—San Luis was gone by 1900. If this was the city of San Luis, he had to be back in the nineteenth century! Now the wagon, the buggy and all the people in Victorian costumes made sense. He wondered what these people might think if they saw Treasure Island today, built where the city of San Luis used to be . . . and now with houses built sixteen feet off the ground.

Alex watched a woman cross the street from the general store to the *San Luis Advocate* newspaper offices. He felt a sudden excitement as he studied her outfit. She wore a long black dress with a full skirt and long sleeves. On her head was a black bonnet trimmed with lacy ribbon, and tied in a big bow under her chin. She was dressed completely in black, just as the ghost had been, and with that same huge bow under her chin. Oh, how he wished Juliann were here to witness this! Could this be the same lady?

Alex positioned himself where she would walk right by him and called, "Ma'am, excuse me, ma'am. Could you help me, please?"

As he expected, she looked straight through him and walked up the steps into the *San Luis Advocate* office. He followed her through the door and stood in the back corner. There, on the wall next to him, a copy of the day's newspaper was pinned to a board. Alex gulped when he read the date at the top: August 26, 1840. He was probably not far from where his beach house was now, but 170 years in the past!

The man behind the counter tucked his pocket watch into the pocket of his striped waistcoat. "Good morning, Mrs. Follett. It is so nice to see you today. It is such a fine morning, is it not?"

"Follett? Did he just say Follett—like in Follett's Island?" Alex muttered.

Mrs. Follett pulled off her gloves and laid them carefully on the countertop. "Indeed, Mr. Folsom—such a fine morning that Alexander has once again abandoned his duties and gone in search of buried treasure on the beach. I don't know what to do with the boy!"

Alex gulped. This was unreal! They were talking about a boy with the same first name as him, living in the same place nearly two centuries earlier, searching for buried treasure. Was Mrs. Follett the ghost in the telephone exchange who had accused him of doing the same thing?

"He is seventeen, is he not? Quite a young man, I should say," said Mr. Folsom.

"Indeed, a young man who should be more concerned about working in the family business than searching for buried treasure on the beach. His father could certainly use his help building the steamboat."

"It is quite a project, I hear."

"That it is. I blame old Mr. Morris at the shipyard for filling Alexander's head with stories of pirates."

"Ah, yes . . . old Mr. Morris! That man truly believes that pirates once sailed in this very bay. In his defense, Mrs. Follett, Spanish coins *have* been found on the San Luis shore."

"So I have heard, Mr. Folsom. But Alexander is now involving his younger sister in this escapade. I swear the boy won't stop searching for buried treasure until he finds some."

"Perhaps he might, Mrs. Follett."

She grabbed a copy of the *San Luis Advocate* from the counter and paid for it. "And perhaps he might not!" she replied indignantly. "Good day, Mr. Folsom!"

"And a very good day to you, Mrs. Follett," he replied as she flounced out.

Alex followed her back down the street. She stopped frequently to talk to people along the way. They walked several blocks and, just after they crossed Orange Street, she turned and walked up the path of a wooden two-story yellow house. It was elaborately decorated, with white verandahs on both floors and a pretty front garden. She climbed the steps and sat on a rocking chair close to the front door.

Alex wondered what he should do next. He realized that his leg hurt. He looked down at the gash on his shin and remembered his fall from the telephone exchange. In his excitement he had forgotten about the pain. The wound was quite deep, but at least the bleeding had almost stopped.

His thoughts were broken by shouting.

"Ma! Ma!" A young girl raced down the street towards him, holding on to her bonnet with one hand and lifting her ankle-length dress with the other. She bolted up the front steps and breathlessly continued, "Ma . . . you just will not believe it!"

"Juliann! What is it, my child?"

Juliann? Alex freaked out. This was totally weird!

"Alexander found some treasure! I told you he would! You should see Ma—he found some gold coins!"

Mrs. Follett frowned and got to her feet. "Such nonsense, Juliann! It's probably a coin or two that someone from San Luis dropped on the beach. Now go inside, Juliann, and wash your hands."

"But, Ma . . ."

"Do not argue with me, daughter!" Mrs. Follett took a last look down the street, as if she were hoping to see someone, and then went inside, slamming the door behind her.

Alex sat down on the top step of the Folletts' front porch, alone with his thoughts. So Juliann was Mrs.

Follett's daughter and Alexander was her son. It seemed too much of a coincidence that his own name was also Alex and that Juliann was his friend in Treasure Island.

The more he found out about Mrs. Follett, the more he was convinced that he had found their ghost. And as for Cabeza de Vaca's treasure . . . according to Juliann Follett, Alexander had found gold coins! Could Cabeza de Vaca have hidden gold, and not sapphires? "I must find Alexander. I've got to see this treasure!" said Alex, staggering to his feet.

He hobbled down the path just as a tall teenage boy ran straight past him, up the steps and through the front door. "That's got to be him!" said Alex, turning straight back around and stumbling back up the steps onto the front porch. "He looks about seventeen. That's gotta be Alexander."

Alex tried to follow him through the front door, but it was now locked. "Dang!" he grumbled. "I've got to find out if Alexander really did find treasure!"

Alex heard shouting inside. It was coming from somewhere close to the front door. He limped over to one of the downstairs windows and peered into an elegantly decorated family room.

Mrs. Follett was standing in the middle of the room, wagging her finger and shouting at her son. Her face was beet red and she looked as though she was about to explode. Then, her son whipped out a small brown pouch from his trouser pocket and dangled it by a long cord in front of her.

Alex was so excited he could hardly breathe. "It's the brown pouch! " he shouted. "Alexander Follett's got Cabeza de Vaca's pouch! Unreal!"

Mrs. Follett swiped at the pouch, knocking it out of her son's hand. Alexander looked horrified. He grabbed the pouch off the floor and came running out the front door.

The door slammed behind him.

Alex, still stunned by what he had just witnessed through the window, took a moment to register that Alexander was now tearing down the street. "Dang!" he grumbled again. "Gotta catch up with him!"

He couldn't lose him—otherwise how would he know what Alexander Follett did with Cabeza de Vaca's treasure? This was the missing link in his puzzle!

Alex winced in pain as he ran down the path and onto Liberty Street. Where had Alexander gone? He seemed to have disappeared! Was that him in the distance, running toward South Street and the ferry? Yes, it was! Could he catch up?

Before Alex knew what was happening, he heard the thundering of carriage wheels, the neighing of horses and the lashing of a whip. He turned around just in time to see a huge carriage pulled by a team of horses heading straight for him.

"Whoa!" he screamed, throwing himself to one side for the second time that day. He hit the ground hard.

"Ahhhhhh!" He writhed in agony. He felt as though he had broken every bone in his body. Was it his old wounds that hurt, or yet more new ones? It was too hard to tell! He lay there looking up at the blue sky in a complete daze. His head pounded, his eyelids felt heavy. "Gotta stay awake . . . gotta catch Alexander," he mumbled. But no matter how hard he tried, he couldn't keep his eyes open.

Finally he gave in and closed his eyes.

Chapter 11

Alex felt someone shaking him. "Gotta catch him," he mumbled.

"Alex! Dude, are you okay? You're not making any sense!"

He squinted in the bright light, trying to work out who was peering over him. "Is it daytime?"

"It's dark, of course, you dummy! It's after midnight!"

"Juliann? Is that you?"

"'Course it's me. You're a mess as usual, Alex Glass!"

"You're blinding me with the flashlight!"

"Oh, sorry," she said as she turned the flashlight away from him. "What happened to you?"

"Not sure," Alex replied, struggling to sit up. He looked around and sighed with relief when he saw the telephone exchange and the brightly colored beach houses.

He touched his head. "Ouch!"

Juliann helped him to his feet. "So what did you do *this* time?" she asked.

"You sound like my mom," said Alex.

"Sorry, but it is a perfectly good question. You should see what you look like right now—and I'm looking at you in the dark!"

Alex sighed. "I guess."

"You still haven't answered me," Juliann pressed. "What *did* you do?"

"I think I fell from up there," said Alex, pointing to the balcony of the telephone exchange.

"Seriously, dude?"

"Seriously," replied Alex. He groaned as he tried to stand without her support.

"You were trying to see the ghost lady again, weren't you?"

"And you weren't?" Alex retorted. "I mean, what else would you be doing out here at this time of night?"

"You got me," she replied.

"I thought you were really scared when we saw her."

"I was . . . I am . . . sort of."

"So what made you come back . . . and on your own, too?"

"I couldn't sleep, thinking about her and wondering what she wanted. I mean, did she want us to go up the tower? And she didn't want to hurt us or anything, did she?"

"No," said Alex, wondering if he should tell her what had happened when he saw the ghost lady a second time.

"Then I saw a light outside my bedroom window," Juliann continued. "When I looked through the curtains I saw you walking away. I just couldn't let you see her again and not be there to see her myself, could I?"

"I guess," said Alex. He took a tiny step and groaned again.

Juliann shone the light on his shin. "Have you seen your leg? It's pouring blood!"

"I know," said Alex, having a flashback of hobbling down the dirt roads in San Luis. "*And* I hit my head again . . . *and* I've got bruises all down my back and chest."

"Your mom will freak out! She'll ground you, dude!"

"She won't know, if you don't tell her," said Alex.

"Really? And how d'you think you're going to hide it from her? You can hardly walk!"

"I'll be fine in the morning."

"Yeah, right!"

"Will you help me up the steps to Island Sapphire?"

"'Course I will, but your mom's going to see you in the morning, you know."

"I'll sleep in late," said Alex.

Juliann laughed. "And what about the next five days while your leg heals? You can't stay in bed for five days!"

"I'll think of something," said Alex, trying to sound confident. Deep down he wondered what on earth he could possibly do to hide his injuries. He couldn't stay in bed for long—he had information to research and treasure to find!

They started to walk back to the beach house. Alex put his arm over Juliann's shoulder for support and hobbled along. They didn't speak for a while. Alex was waiting for her to ask the obvious question. He knew he was tormenting her by saying nothing.

Finally she blurted out, "So, dude, *did* you see the ghost lady again? Is that why you fell?"

Alex looked at her for a minute and then said, "I've got a lot to tell you, but I don't want you to get scared, or anything."

"Who me?" she said with a giggle.

"Yeah, you," said Alex. "Miss, 'I love snakes and spiders' Fownes."

"Okay, okay. You can laugh at me, Alex Glass. I've got over the shock of seeing a ghost, I promise. At least you know I'll believe you a hundred percent now."

"Well, some really weird stuff happened," said Alex. "And I mean *really* weird . . ."

"Go on then!" she snapped. "Did you see her?"

"Yes, I saw the ghost lady. Her name is Mrs. Follett."

"Mrs. Follett," repeated Juliann. "Like in Follett's Island?"

"I guess they're connected," said Alex. "Anyway, she thought that I was her son, Alexander, and that you were her daughter, Juliann."

"What?" Juliann cried. "Really?"

"Really. It's pretty weird that we've got the same names as her kids, don't you think?"

"Yeah. So how did you fall?"

"She sort of came at me . . ."

"Came at you? Came at you how? Now you *are* scaring me!"

"I don't think she meant to hurt me. She thought I was her son and she yelled at me for looking for buried treasure when I was supposed to be looking after you. She was worried because she couldn't find you. She was telling me off and wagging her finger at me. I stepped back to get out of her way and I fell backwards down the staircase."

"Ouch!" Juliann sympathized.

"The buried treasure bit is weird too, don't you think?"

Juliann nodded. "I mean, how would she know you've been looking for Cabeza de Vaca's buried treasure?"

"I don't know . . . how do ghosts know anything? There's a whole lot more that happened," said Alex.

"More?" She stopped him in the middle of the road. "What more could there be?"

"Remember how I saw Cabeza de Vaca and his men on the beach of Malhado? Well, I also saw our ghost lady in San Luis."

"San Luis?"

"Remember how Suzan told us that Treasure Island is built where the city of San Luis used to be, and that's why the area is called San Luis Pass today? Well, there I was in San Luis in 1840.   I swear!   I saw a copy of the *San Luis Advocate* newspaper and read the date on it."

"How does this happen to you?"

Alex shrugged. "I don't know. I don't know how it happens.   It almost feels like I'm in a dream, but everything is so clear and it's like I'm really there. I can see the people, hear their conversations, and I'm walking down the streets with them, too. I can even smell the sea and the food they eat."

"Wow!" said Juliann, fixated on him.

"And d'you know what happened this time?"

"Don't keep me waiting!"

"I saw our ghost lady in her house on Liberty Street with her daughter Juliann and her son Alexander. You'll never guess what he had . . ."

"What? Tell me!"

"Cabeza de Vaca's brown pouch—the one that I saw him bury on San Luis Island!"

"For real?"

"For real.   So tomorrow I want to find out everything I can about San Luis Island in 1840. Everything I saw happen on the beach with Cabeza de Vaca really happened in history, so I want to see if all the stuff I saw this time is real too."

"Not *all* the stuff with Cabeza de Vaca was real," said Juliann. "The treasure part might not be. There's no proof that Cabeza de Vaca ever had sapphires that he gave to the Indians, or that he had any other treasure that he buried."

"Yeah, I know," said Alex glumly. "But I saw him hide the pouch and I also saw Alexander with it. I believe the treasure is real and I'm going to find it if it kills me!"

They reached the bottom of the beach house steps. Juliann helped Alex slowly up to the top.

"You'll tell me *every* little detail tomorrow, right?" she whispered.

"I promise," said Alex. "Just don't expect to see me until noon!"

"What's new?" she laughed quietly.

"Can you do me a favor, Juliann?"

"Sure . . . name it."

"Will you call Suzan and ask her if we can go to the museum tomorrow afternoon? I've got to know if what happened tonight is true."

"Sure. I'll text you about the time." She left him at the front door and disappeared down the steps.

Alex hobbled into the beach house and straight to the bathroom, where he struggled to take off his clothes.

He was in agony with every movement of his shoulder or leg. He bathed his leg, clenching his teeth every time he touched the wound. Getting into bed was even harder, especially as he was trying not to make any sounds that would wake Joe. He wondered how he could possibly fool his mom in the morning when he was so badly bruised. He'd think of something . . . he had to! Being grounded wasn't an option right now. He had too much to do.

Chapter 12

Alex was vaguely aware that his cell phone was going off—playing that annoying melody that he still hadn't got around to changing. Juliann would have to wait. He needed his sleep.

His mom stormed into the room and turned off his phone. "Alex! What *is* the matter with you this morning!" she yelled. "Actually, it's the afternoon! It's nearly one o'clock, you're still in bed, and your phone has been ringing constantly for the last hour."

She bent over his bed to reprimand him further.

Alex quickly pulled the covers up around his neck to hide the bruises. "I'm so tired. I guess I'm still recovering from my fall."

"I don't mind if you want to sleep in, Alex, but *please* turn your phone off in the future! It's been driving me crazy!"

"Sorry, Mom. I'll turn it off next time, I promise."

"Now call Juliann, will you? It's bound to be her."

"Sure."

His mom started for the door.

"Mom . . ." Alex called after her. "Can I go to the Surfside Museum with Juliann and Mrs. Zachariah this afternoon? Mrs. Zachariah's been telling us the history of Treasure Island. Did you know that Cabeza de Vaca landed here in 1528 when it was called San Luis Island?"

His mom looked surprised. "No, I didn't know. Nor did I know that you were interested in that kind of stuff." She gave him a beaming smile. "Of course you can go—it sounds like a great idea. I actually think you'll be doing something very useful for once . . . and just maybe you'll stay out of trouble," she muttered as she shut his bedroom door.

Alex tried to sit up. He was so stiff that he could hardly reach for the phone. Juliann had left him three texts: 'mrs z will take us at 2', 'going at 2' and 'can u be ready by 2?'

Alex texted her back. 'just got up. c u at 2.' He looked at his bedside clock. It was already 1:10 p.m. That didn't leave him much time!

He struggled into the bathroom, grabbing his only pair of khakis from his closet on the way. They would hide the gash on his leg — and going to the museum was a good excuse to wear them without his mom being suspicious.

It took him much longer than normal to shower and get ready. He looked in the bathroom mirror when he was dressed. "You're a mess, Alex Glass," he said, imitating Juliann. But she was right — he *was* in a pretty bad state. Fortunately his face was okay, his mom already knew about the bruises on his arm, and the recent injuries were hidden by his clothing. If he could hide his pain then just maybe he could get away with last night's adventure.

He had one more thing to do before he faced his mom. He took out a pad of paper and a pen from the drawer of his bedside cabinet. What could he remember from being in San Luis in 1840 that he could check in a museum? He had to make a list if he wanted to prove that it had really happened.

"Think, Alex, think . . . first there was the wagon and later the buggy thingy." He began scribbling down everything he could recall.

1. *Transportation and clothing in 1840*
2. *San Luis Advocate — Liberty Street and Market Street*

3. *Houses, buildings and streets in San Luis — South Street, Liberty Street, Market Street. Bennett's hotel.*
4. *Follett family — Mrs. Follett, Alexander and Juliann lived on Liberty Street between Center Street and Orange Street.*
5. *Ferry?*

"Done. That'll work," he said, folding the piece of paper and shoving it in his back pocket.

He drew in a deep breath, put a big smile on his face and tried to walk upright into the kitchen.

His mom looked at him with a curious expression. Alex felt suddenly hot. Had she already worked out that something was wrong?

But then she commented, "You look very smart today," and gave him another beaming smile. Alex sighed with relief. She had been so occupied by the fact that he'd dressed up to go to the museum that she hadn't noticed anything else.

"Got to go, Mom. Mrs. Zachariah is collecting us at two." He quickly headed for the kitchen door.

"Here, eat this on the way," she said, thrusting a sandwich at him. "Otherwise — I know you — you'll be buying junk food later."

"Thanks, Mom. See you tonight."

"Be good!"

Yeah, right, thought Alex. That would mean no more ghost hunting or treasure hunting, and that wasn't about to happen!

Once he got out of her sight, he relaxed and allowed himself to grip the handrail as he walked slowly down the steps. Suzan was waiting in the car with Juliann. He opened the front passenger door, feeling the pain as he twisted to get in.

"Hi, Alex," said Suzan.

"Hello, ma'am." He pulled the safety belt across his body, flinching as it tightened.

Suzan drove off, soon passing the telephone exchange at the entrance to Treasure Island. She smiled at Alex and said, "Juliann's been telling me about last night's escapades. You seem to be suffering just a little today."

"Yes, ma'am, just a little, but it was worth it."

"I'm glad you think so," she replied, obviously trying to contain a laugh.

Juliann was giggling in the back, and before long, Alex was laughing too, even though it killed him to do so. Every time he moved, the muscles between his ribs hurt.

"Juliann told me that you saw another ghost, but that she was with you this time."

"Yes, ma'am. We call her the ghost lady. She was on the balcony of the telephone exchange."

"She also said that you had quite an experience in the city of San Luis."

"Experience? I guess that's a good word for it. I wouldn't know what else to call it. But whatever—it was unbelievable!" said Alex. "Now I have to find out if all the things I saw and heard really are true."

"Well, I think we should go straight to the Brazoria County Museum. They have so much information on San Luis Island."

"Great!" said Alex.

Suzan turned out of the neighborhood and onto Bluewater Highway. Alex squirmed in his seat, trying to get comfortable for the ride.

Chapter 13

Suzan pulled into the parking lot of the Brazoria County Historical Museum in Angleton. It was an impressive large, gray stucco building with a cream-colored stone trim and lots of long rectangular windows.

"We have to go in at the side entrance as they're renovating the building right now," she said. "It'll be really nice when it is finished."

"How old is this place?" asked Alex.

"It was built in 1897 and used to be the court house. It didn't look like this back then. They renovated the building in 1927."

Alex hobbled up the ramp behind Suzan and Juliann. Inside the door was a temporary reception area. Suzan asked if they could speak to the curator of the museum, and the lady at the desk directed them upstairs.

They passed empty rooms that were about to be renovated and several men who were painting the green trim around the doors in the hallway. Alex lagged behind climbing up the iron steps to the second floor. Finally they reached an office door that read 'Curator,' and stepped inside.

"Hello, Michael," said Suzan. "I've brought a couple of my young friends to meet you. This is Alex Glass and Juliann Fownes."

Michael got out of his chair to greet them. He was a large jolly man with long hair tied back in a braid. "Come in, come in and welcome! You've both got great names," he added.

"We have?" Alex wondered what he meant by that, but just as Michael started to explain, Juliann shrieked, "This place is awesome!"

"There's a gold mine of information in here," said Michael. "So how can I help you kids?"

Alex looked around, amazed at the masses of books and literature stacked in piles all around the room. He wondered how Michael knew where everything was.

"I have a lot of questions about San Luis Island," said Alex, pulling out the piece of paper from his pocket. "Have you got any information about that, please?"

Michael laughed. "How long do you want to spend here?"

"Really?" asked Alex. "You've got that much?"

"You could be here for days!" said Michael. "We have *so* much information on San Luis Island—where would you like to start? Come and meet my assistant, Jamie, and she'll help you find what you need."

He showed them through an archway into the next room.

"Wow!" said Alex. He could tell from Juliann's expression that she was as stunned as he was by the piles of books and papers stacked on the floor and on the shelves. On one side of the room was a computer and a photocopier, and at the other end of the room sat a heavy wooden chest of drawers. There were filing cabinets full of information, and even the large table in the middle of the room was partially covered with books and folders.

Jamie appeared from a side room. She was a middle-aged lady with a warm welcoming smile, dressed elegantly in a long skirt. She took off her glasses and asked how she could help him.

Alex studied her friendly face and wondered if he dared tell her about his experiences with ghosts. Juliann and Suzan were busy talking with Michael, so he quietly said to Jamie, "My family has a beach house on Follett's Island. Do you think there might be ghosts in my neighborhood of Treasure Island, in San Luis Pass?"

"Oh, it's *quite* possible," she responded and ushered him to the big table. "There are several people who say they have seen a ghost near the San Luis Pass Bridge."

"Ma'am, that's right next to Treasure Island! I can see the bridge from our beach house."

"The story is that the ghost is a woman whose children drowned in a boating accident in the strong currents beneath the bridge, and so now she searches for them every night."

"That's sad."

She nodded. "Yes, it is. I can tell you many tales of ghosts in Brazoria County. You should read *Ghosts along the Brazos* by Catherine Munson Foster. She has recorded fourteen accounts of ghosts in Brazoria County."

"That's a lot. I want to find out about San Luis Island because I have seen two ghosts . . . no, actually, five ghosts," Alex blurted out.

"Five? When?" Jamie asked.

"Yesterday, and the day before, and a couple days before that."

She raised her eyebrows. "Yesterday?"

"But then strange things seem to happen to me. I see things that happened to these ghosts during their lifetimes—and I know it's not stuff I have read on the internet or learned in school."

Jamie looked surprised, but not disbelieving, so Alex continued. "The first ghost I saw was Cabeza de Vaca... and then once I saw three of his men with him. We worked out who he was because he kept calling 'Malhado' and he showed me the skull of a cow. Everything I saw happen to him and everything I heard him say checks out, so now I want to find out more about the ghost lady too."

Jamie was on the edge of her chair. "Cabeza de Vaca? Very interesting! That's a long time in the past."

"1528," said Alex.

Jamie nodded. "Indeed. So, tell me more about the ghost lady, then."

"She was dressed all in black with a dress puffed out with petticoats. She had this lacy bonnet with a big bow tied under her chin. Her name was Mrs. Follett."

"Follett? Now you really have got my interest!"

"Really?"

"How did you find out her name?"

"I heard the guy in the *San Luis Advocate* office call her that." Alex slid the piece of paper with his list across the table toward her. "I'm trying to work out if there was a Mrs. Follett in San Luis, Texas, and if everything I saw and heard was true."

Jamie studied the list for a second and beamed at him. "I can answer all of these questions!"

"You can?" Alex was nearly off his chair.

"You wait until you see what I've got in here!" She walked over to a filing cabinet near the door and pulled out a fat manila folder that was overflowing with sheets of paper. She laid it on the table in front of him. "Open it and take a look," she instructed. "Juliann and Suzan should see this too."

She interrupted their conversation with Michael and called all three of them over. They all stood behind Alex, looking over his shoulder.

Alex took out the first sheet of paper. There was a photograph of a man with a long gray beard dressed in Victorian clothing, and alongside was an article about him. "Alexander Glass Follett," he read from underneath the photograph. He looked up at Jamie in disbelief. "Dang! So there really was an Alexander

Follett! He even has my last name for his middle name — Alexander *Glass* Follett!"

Juliann let out a squeal of excitement.

"Keep reading, Alex," urged Michael.

"Born 1823, died 1906, son of John Bradbury Follett and Anne Louise Fownes. Mrs. Follett's maiden name was Fownes?"

Juliann shrieked. "Fownes? That's my last name! This is so weird!"

"Read on," said Jamie.

"Their children, Alonzo, Joseph, Alexander, Juliann . . ."

"Juliann? She really did have a daughter named Juliann!" said Juliann to Alex.

"Now do you understand why I said that you both had great names?" asked Michael.

"Man, this can't *just* be a coincidence!" said Alex. "Surely this proves we saw Mrs. Follett's ghost. I didn't know any of this!"

"Nor did I," added Juliann.

"Now look at this photo," said Jamie, reaching into the folder. She pulled out a black-and-white photo of a lady wearing a black bonnet with lace trim and a big bow.

"Dang, that's her!" Alex shouted.

"That's our ghost lady, dude!" agreed Juliann.

Suzan had been quiet the whole time. Alex looked at her and saw she had a startled look on her face. "So what do you think?" he asked her.

"What can I say? I'm really starting to believe in ghosts! There seem to be too many coincidences for there not to be some truth to your story."

"Well," said Jamie. "You're going to be blown away by what I am going to show you next. Alex, if you flip through the papers you should see the original plan for the city of San Luis, surveyed in 1840."

"Is this it, ma'am?"

"Yes, that's it. I want you to look at the street names and compare them to those on your list," Jamie instructed.

"See this?" said Alex, pointing to the map, "South Street is right by the coast where I got off the ferry!"

"The Follett family did run a ferry service across Little Pass for many years, and across Big Pass too," said Jamie. "Big Pass is now San Luis Pass."

"This is the place, for sure," said Alex excitedly. "I walked down Liberty Street to Market Street, and the *San Luis Advocate* office was right on the corner."

"Okay," said Jamie. "In the folder you will find some photocopies of pages from the San Luis newspaper. Pull them out."

Alex rifled through until he found them. He was flabbergasted when he read out loud for everyone to hear, "*San Luis Advocate*, the corner of Market and Liberty Streets, San Luis, Texas."

"Dude, I'm totally convinced," said Juliann. "You *really* are seeing these things."

"Dang!" said Alex, at a loss for words.

"Now where was the Folletts' house?" asked Jamie. "Point it out on the map."

"Man, let's think about this a minute," said Alex. "I followed Mrs. Follett quite a way down Liberty Street." He traced his finger along the map as he spoke. "We passed a general store and a hotel, and then we crossed Cherry Street and then Orange Street. Mrs. Follett turned into a house that was here before we got to Center Street."

"Okay," said Jamie. "Everyone see where Alex is pointing on the map? It is in Ward 1, block 22 and lot 3 or 4."

She passed the map around. Juliann took a look and then handed it to Suzan.

Jamie reached across the table to the folder once again, and flipped through until she found yet another photocopy. "Okay, this was written by Fannie Mae Follett Gilbert, who still lives in Lake Jackson. She says that the first recorded history shows John Bradbury as owning lots 3 and 4 in Block 22, First Ward, in the city of San Luis."

Everyone gasped.

Alex was too stunned to say anything.

He felt a cold chill in the room. He wondered if perhaps Mrs. Follett's ghost was standing next to him. He stared at the map on the table. Yes, he had definitely been to San Luis. He could picture the place clearly.

Finally Jamie broke the silence. "I will make you photocopies of these maps," she said. "But first, I've something else I want to show you. It was published in 1853."

She walked over to the big chest at the end of the room, opened the bottom drawer and pulled out a large chart. At the top it said 'San Luis Pass, Texas; Survey of the Coast of Texas.'

"See here?" she said, laying it down on the table for everyone to see. "This was drawn when San Luis Island was separate from the mainland. You can see where it was cut off by the waters of Little Pass. And what do you read here, Alex?" She handed him a magnifying glass.

"Ferry," said Alex. "It says, 'Follett's Ferry'!" He looked first at Juliann and then at Suzan. "Can you believe this stuff?"

"Isn't that about the same place that you caught the ferry across to the city of San Luis?" asked Jamie.

"Man, that's the place, for sure."

"I would say, 'case closed'!" said Jamie, giving him a satisfied smile.

Alex was ecstatic. Surely *everyone* had to believe his stories now! There were just too many things he had got completely right. But there was one more thing he had to ask . . . "Gold coins," he said, his thoughts spilling out. "Ma'am, can you tell me about Spanish coins?"

Jamie looked slightly puzzled. "What time period, Alex?"

"Around November 6, 1528."

"That's the date that Cabeza de Vaca landed on San Luis Island, isn't it?" she queried.

Alex nodded. "I really think that Cabeza de Vaca hid some gold coins on San Luis Island. The first time I saw him, he whispered, 'I cannot rest, I cannot go, while 'tis buried on Malhado.' I saw him hide a brown pouch on the beach. But that part of the beach isn't there anymore."

"You mean because of erosion?"

"Yes, ma'am."

"The coastline of this area certainly has changed a lot since Cabeza de Vaca was here."

"But then in San Luis, I saw Alexander Glass Follett with a brown pouch that looked just the same. He told his mother and sister that he had found treasure on the beach."

"That would have been three hundred years later," said Jamie.

"Yes, ma'am. So what I want to know is, could Cabeza de Vaca have had Spanish coins with him in 1528 when he landed on San Luis Island?"

"Can I cut in here?" Michael asked.

"Sure," said Alex, turning to look at him.

"There are those that would say yes and those that would say no. Don't forget Cabeza de Vaca survived a hurricane to land on our shores and he probably lost everything in the storm."

"But what if he had his treasure tied around his neck in a brown pouch?" asked Alex.

"If you're asking if there were Spanish coins at that time, then the answer is yes," responded Michael. "In fact, Cabeza de Vaca was part of the Narvaez expedition. One of the ships from that expedition was shipwrecked off the coast of Florida, and old Spanish coins do turn up sometimes on the beaches around Port Charlotte."

"No kidding!" said Alex.

Juliann looked at Alex and then back at Michael. Her eyes were wide with excitement. "So Cabeza de Vaca really is telling Alex to find his treasure?"

"Hold on!" said Michael. "We can't jump to that conclusion. It does seem that everything Alex has told us checks out historically, but there are a lot of scientists and historians who would instantly say that he could have found out the information he told us some other way."

"No. No way, man!" said Alex. "I swear . . . it happened just like I told you."

"And I saw the ghost lady too!" said Juliann, looking upset.

"They're not saying that either of you is lying," Suzan explained. "They're just saying that there are many explanations for why people see ghosts."

"You see, kids, Jamie and I know nothing about ghosts—we're both historians. We deal only with historical facts," explained Michael.

"We have to leave ghost hunting to the ghost busters," Jamie added.

Alex couldn't help but smile. He understood where Jamie and Michael were coming from, but he desperately wanted someone to say 'Yes, Alex Glass, you really have seen the ghosts of Malhado.'

Alex was quiet most of the way home. He had forgotten about his injuries the whole time that he was at the Brazoria County Historical Museum, and only now did he notice his throbbing leg and pounding head. The afternoon had been exciting, for sure. He looked at the photocopies on his lap. Everything seemed to fit together. Now all he had to do was work out where Alexander Glass Follett had hidden Cabeza de Vaca's treasure. But how would he do that?

Chapter 14

It was almost dark. Alex lay in the hammock on the back deck of Island Sapphire listening to the sound of the sea. It was calming, especially when his body hurt all over and he was exhausted from putting on a brave face all day. He was a complete mess! He knew that he needed a good night's sleep, but how could he sleep when he was desperate to find the buried treasure? He needed to go ghost hunting again.

But what would be the point? Back in 1840, did Mrs. Follett know what had happened to the treasure after Alexander had it? Alexander Glass Follett was the key, for sure. He was *probably* the last one to see Cabeza de Vaca's treasure. Alex was frustrated. If only he could meet Alexander's ghost!

Juliann appeared at the top of the steps. She took one look at him under the glaring outside lights and said, "Dude, you're a mess!"

"So you keep telling me," said Alex.

"Has your mom said anything about your leg or your bruises?"

"Nah. I've worn pants all day, stayed out of her way, and suffered through the pain to walk properly when she was watching."

"Dang, you're good! Don't think I could have done it."

"It was either that or get grounded."

"I guess."

"She was really interested to hear about Cabeza de Vaca and the Follett family over dinner . . . that distracted her. I even showed her all the copies we had of maps and plans. Of course I didn't tell her about the ghosts and the things I've seen. Mom would freak out. She'd be really worried every time I went out the door."

" — and that would be another reason for grounding you," Juliann added. "Moms are over protective. I'd probably get grounded for going with you."

Alex laughed. "Yeah, you would. Your mom's just as bad as mine." He groaned as he swung his legs over the edge of the hammock and walked across the deck to a seat. At least he was walking again and not hobbling everywhere.

"I've got to find that treasure, Juliann," he said as he lowered himself into a comfy chair. "We go home next week so that Dad can go to the office and do some work. We don't come back to Treasure Island until the middle of July. I can't wait until then to carry on the search. It would kill me!"

"Got any great ideas?"

Alex shook his head. "Not right now. If only I could see Alexander Glass Follett. Perhaps I could find out what he did with the treasure!"

"Seriously, dude. You don't really want to injure yourself any more, do you?"

Alex shrugged. "So what do we do to find it?"

"Do you think you can walk a short way?"

"Why? You got an idea?" Alex asked excitedly.

"No, but we can get some candy from the Bright Light while we think of one."

"Awww . . . I thought for a minute you had a good idea."

"I always get good ideas when I eat," said Juliann.

Alex groaned—she was always eating. "Okay, but don't blame me if you have to carry me back!"

Alex found that going down the steps was getting easier. Perhaps by tomorrow he'd be back up to speed. They took their usual route through the neighborhood, down Palm Avenue and past the telephone exchange at the entrance. Alex paused for a second to look up at the balcony. Juliann tugged at his shirt.

"Seriously, dude. Leave it for one night," she begged. "Get over these injuries first, will you!"

They crossed Bluewater Highway and approached the yellow store, which, like all the buildings in the area, sat sixteen feet off the ground on pilings. There was a long ramp up to the door.

Alex looked up at the sign on the front of the store, brightly lit for all to read. "The Bright Lite," he said, starting up the ramp. "Hmm. L-i-t-e. I never knew that was how the name was spelled." Then he stopped dead. "Hang on, Juliann!" He almost ran down the ramp in excitement and looked up at the sign again. "The Bright Lite! That's it!"

"What's it?" asked Juliann. "What are you talking about?"

"The Bright Lite!" he shouted again. "That's what Cabeza de Vaca wrote in the sand!"

"He did?"

"Yeah! He wrote 'Bright is the Lite of Malhado.' He spelled the word 'light' l-i-t-e. I thought he had misspelled light, but he was leaving me a clue, I'm sure of it!" He pointed to the sign above the door. "Look how Light is spelled L-i-t-e on the sign."

"Oh . . . so it is," said Juliann.

"All the times I've got candy from here and I never noticed that before," said Alex.

"Me neither."

"That's got to be a clue, don't you think?"

"I guess," said Juliann. "But what does it mean?"

Alex stared up at the sign and thought for a minute. "I think I might know," he finally said. "The maps—I've got to go back to Island Sapphire and look at the maps we got from the Brazoria County Historical Museum."

"Okay. Why?"

"I'll show you when we get there," said Alex.

"Can I get my candy first?"

Alex frowned at her. "I'll wait here. I've got some thinking to do." He watched her run up the ramp. Candy! Who needed candy when there was treasure to find?

Chapter 15

"Dang, which one was it?" Alex muttered. He spread the photocopies from the Brazoria County Historical Museum across the kitchen table. "Here! This is it!"

"What are you looking for?" asked Juliann, chomping on a candy bar.

"Remember this? This is the survey of the Texas coast from 1853. See — Follett's Ferry is labeled." He pointed to the dotted line between San Luis Island and the mainland. "That's where the ferry went across Little Pass."

"So?" said Juliann.

"Now look at this map. This is what it's like here now. There's no San Luis Island anymore. Little Pass got silted up and San Luis Island is now joined to Follett's Island. The red box shows exactly where San Luis Island used to be."

Juliann pulled a face at him. "So?" she said again. "I don't get it."

"Don't you see? It's Treasure Island! San Luis Island was located *exactly* where our neighborhood has been built."

"Yeah, sure, I see that. But seriously, dude, didn't we already know that from Suzan? And I still don't get how this helps us find the treasure," said Juliann.

"A lot of the coast has been eroded, but look in the red box at where Bluewater Highway is."

"Okay, Bluewater Highway is about where San Luis Island got joined to the mainland at Little Pass."

"Exactly!"

"Just spit it out, Alex. Enough with the riddle! Tell me what you're thinking, for cryin' out loud!"

"The Bright Lite is on Bluewater Highway. I think Follett's Ferry used to be where the Bright Lite is now!"

Juliann peered at the map. "Dang! Could be!"

"I saw Alexander Glass Follett running down Liberty Street towards the ferry, carrying Cabeza de Vaca's pouch. His family owned and ran the ferry. I'm betting that since his mom was against him treasure hunting, he couldn't keep the treasure at home . . ."

". . . so he buried it somewhere near the family ferry," finished Juliann.

"Exactly. So the treasure has got to be somewhere near the Bright Lite, and that's what Cabeza de Vaca was telling me!"

"I hate to remind you, Alex, but it's all critter-infested saltwater marsh around the Bright Lite. Just how do you think we're going to find treasure in that lot? I'm not wading into the marsh!"

"And neither am I," said Alex. "But we might get lucky. The treasure might be close to the Bright Lite or buried somewhere in the neighborhood."

"But Alex . . . the treasure is going to be *buried*. You just said it yourself. It's not going to be lying on the surface. We still need a clue as to exactly where to dig."

Alex sighed. "I know."

"Unless . . ."

"Unless what?"

"Don't move!" said Juliann. "I'll be right back."

She ran out of the kitchen, leaving Alex dumbfounded. He stood there for a second, staring after her, and then decided to study the maps one more time to check his theory.

A few minutes later, Juliann came flying back through the kitchen door carrying a strange contraption rather like a string trimmer. It was a long pole with a large black box and a handle at the top, and a circular disc on the bottom.

"Here . . . it's my dad's!" she announced.

"What is it?" asked Alex.

"It's a metal detector, dummy!"

"No kiddin'? That's awesome! Does it work?"

"Sure! It's an expensive one, too. My dad sometimes walks along the beach with it, pulling up stuff. He's never found anything really valuable—it's usually trashy bits of metal—but he has found a couple of quarters. So, it might help us find the treasure."

Alex's mom walked into the kitchen and loaded some plates into the dishwasher. "Hi, Juliann."

"Hi, Mrs. Glass."

"Oh, you've got a metal detector," she said.

"It's my dad's."

"Are you going treasure hunting?"

"Maybe," said Alex. "We might try looking tomorrow. There's supposed to be Jean Lafitte's treasure in Galveston Bay somewhere." Alex felt bad for lying to his mom, but he didn't want her worrying.

His mom laughed. "I'm sorry," she said. "I don't mean to laugh—and I wish you luck with your treasure hunting—but just because we have a beach house in Treasure Island doesn't mean you're going to find treasure here!"

"We know, Mom," said Alex, rolling his eyes.

"Remember, there's *always* talk of pirate treasure in any coastal community, and everyone hopes that they will be the lucky one to find it, but rarely is it found."

"We know, Mom," said Alex again.

Alex's mom went back to her TV program.

Alex turned to Juliann and said, "But what she doesn't know is that *we've* got a head start."

Juliann checked her cell. "It's 9:30. I've got to go." She balanced the metal detector against the wall by the back door. "Okay if I leave this here for the morning?"

"Sure," said Alex.

"I'll be back at nine tomorrow. Can you be up by then?"

"I can be up *before* then," said Alex. "Tomorrow I've got something to get up for!"

Alex shut the kitchen door after her and went to his room. He left the bedroom light off so that he could look out of the window. He stood in the quiet of the bedroom staring across Bluewater Highway. The lights from the Bright Lite twinkled in the distance, just like they had the night before. But this time it seemed as if they were calling to him.

Suddenly he felt a cold chill in the room. How strange! He was sure it wasn't the air conditioning blowing at him. He shivered and went to rub his arms, but then remembered the bruises.

"Bright is the Lite of Malhado," came a whisper.

Alex swallowed hard. He pressed his nose up to the glass, feeling both excited and scared. Was the ghost of Cabeza de Vaca standing below? He couldn't see anything. It was probably just his brain working overtime after everything that he had found out about San Luis. He couldn't wait for tomorrow so that he could get started with his treasure hunting! How could he sleep tonight?

"Malhado! Malhado! My San Luis Isle!" The sorrowful call was loud and clear.

Alex spun around, half expecting to see Cabeza de Vaca standing in his bedroom, but he wasn't there. Now his heart was racing. He desperately wanted to see the ghost again, but he wondered if he would ever *not* be frightened first.

"Malhado! 'Tis buried on Malhado."

Where was the sound coming from? Alex crept up to his closet. He hesitated in front of the closet door. His palms sweated as he slowly turned the handle. Was Cabeza de Vaca's ghost inside?

The door creaked as Alex opened it . . . first an inch, then two . . . then three. He waited for flashes of light, but there were none. Perhaps Suzan and his dad had been right, and the flashes had nothing to do with the ghosts.

He took a step forward and slowly peered inside . . . he couldn't see anything. He gulped as he moved the clothes to one side . . . nothing but clothes and smelly shoes!

He sighed with relief, but then felt disappointed.

"Enough already!" he told himself. "Switch your brain off ghosts for one night!"

He walked over to his bed, pulled his boxer shorts from under his pillow and started to undress. But just as he pulled his T-shirt over his head, he heard tapping on the window.

Alex spun around. The large sunken eyes of Cabeza de Vaca's ghost glared at him through the glass.

"Ahhhh!" Alex screamed and jumped back in surprise—even though he had prepared himself for the ghostly encounter.

"Alexander Glasssssssss." The whisper seemed to linger forever.

"Y-Y- Yes . . . it . . . it's me," stammered Alex.

"Help me rest, help me go.
Find what's buried on Malhado.
But what you find, leave behind
On my sweet San Luis Isle."

"Yes, yes . . . I promise," whispered Alex.

Light suddenly flooded through the bedroom door.

"Alex! Alex!"

"Mom?" said Alex, turning to the door. He realized he was shaking.

"Are you okay?" His mom entered the room. "I thought I heard you scream."

"I thought I saw . . ." Alex looked back at the window. The ghost of Cabeza de Vaca had gone.

"You thought you saw what?"

"Oh, nothing," said Alex. She'd never *ever* believe him.

"Well, if you're sure you're all right . . ."

"I'm fine, thanks, Mom. I'm going to bed."

"It's early for you, isn't it?"

"I'm tired," said Alex, which was true.

"Okay. Joe's coming to bed right now. Have a good night, dear."

She closed the door, leaving Alex alone in the dark. He sat down on his bunk, excited, scared and yet nervous all at once. Cabeza de Vaca wanted him to find his treasure, for sure. But what did he mean about leaving it behind?

Alex got up to close the curtains. The window seemed to have steamed up. He swallowed hard. Scrawled across the glass was a name in cursive writing:

Álvar Núñez Cabeza de Vaca.

Chapter 16

Early morning was usually Alex's favorite time of the day, especially at Island Sapphire. But this morning Alex wasn't feeling so happy. He stood on the front deck watching the brown pelicans flying in formation along the sea front, and the fishermen casting their lines into the surf. Today everyone in Treasure Island seemed to be happy—even the panting joggers smiled and waved as they passed the house—but Alex felt depressed.

His brain had been working overtime ever since Cabeza de Vaca's ghost had revisited him last night. In the back of his mind he kept hearing, 'But what you find, leave behind on my sweet San Luis Isle.' It was like a song that had got stuck in his head and was playing over and over. He just couldn't shake it off. He had lain awake for hours thinking about it. What did the rhyme mean? And that wasn't all he was worried about. He couldn't wait to start looking for the treasure—but would they actually find it? He felt sure that the chances were slim. If they didn't find it, would Cabeza de Vaca's ghost haunt him forever? He shuddered. The thought was too scary! And then there was that other small problem—what to do with the treasure if they *did* find it!

He checked his cell. No text from Juliann. Where was she? Hadn't they agreed on 9 a.m.? It was 8:55. Juliann was usually early. They had to get started because it was going to be another hot day.

Finally she appeared on the deck.

"There you are!" said Alex. She was dressed in a pink T-shirt with matching pink ribbons, and her hair was neatly braided. "I can see what took you so long!" he added.

"Dude, seriously! I'm *still* early!" she said, as if she had read his mind. "You're a mess as usual—you look like you haven't even *combed* your hair."

"I didn't sleep much."

"It shows."

"Thanks," said Alex. "I kept wondering about where we should start looking. I mean, *really* . . . what are the chances that we'll find any treasure?"

"'Slim to none,' my mom always says when Dad goes out with the metal detector. And so far she's right—he hasn't found any treasure yet."

"Yeah—the chance of us finding anything . . ."

"Dude, it sounds like you're giving up before we've even started!"

"No . . . no, I'm not. I'm just trying to be realistic," said Alex, grabbing the metal detector from outside the back door. "I've got two bottles of water and a spade too," he said, picking them up off the deck and handing her the spade and one bottle to carry. "Though I don't know how much digging I can do with this leg and my bruised arms."

Alex found himself ambling along Palm Avenue, his thoughts still tormenting him. He wished he could feel more excited about searching for the treasure.

The Bright Lite was busy. The parking lot out front was full with cars and pick-up trucks towing boats. Debbie, the manager, was running up and down the stairs getting bait for the Saturday morning fishermen. She waved at them as they approached, and shouted over the railing, "Hey kids, what you got there?"

"It's a metal detector . . . it's for finding treasure," Juliann yelled back.

"Hope you'll share it with me when you get rich!" She laughed loudly and went back inside the store.

Her comments made Alex feel even more deflated. "No one thinks we'll find anything," he said glumly.

"And why should they?" said Juliann. "No one else has found treasure around here. But remember that no one knows about the ghosts you've seen. What's up with you this morning, Alex? You're in a really strange mood."

Alex hesitated and then decided he had to tell her. After all, he'd told her everything else. "I saw the ghost of Cabeza de Vaca again last night. He called to me and then I saw him looking through my bedroom window."

"Dude . . . that's unreal! Why didn't you say something sooner?"

Alex shrugged. "He said some weird stuff and it has me a bit spooked, I guess."

"What weird stuff?"

"Well, he said, 'Help me rest, help me go. Find what's buried on Malhado. But what you find, leave behind on my sweet San Luis Isle.'"

Juliann frowned. "What's that supposed to mean?"

"Dunno. I told you it was weird. He wants me to find the treasure but then leave it here? I don't get it. What am I supposed to do with it?"

"Well, let's find it first. If we don't find anything you won't have to worry about it!"

"True," said Alex. He took the spade from Juliann and handed her the metal detector. "Okay, it's already getting hot and I'm still having to wear pants, so let's get looking. Turn this thing on and show me how it works."

"I hope the battery is okay. See . . . you turn it on at the top here and adjust this dial for sensitivity."

"Sensitivity? What's that?" asked Alex.

"It means that you can tune it to the size and type of metal you want."

"So, like, we want gold because we're looking for gold coins."

"Right. Then it will beep and show up on this display here if we get a hit."

"A hit?"

Juliann groaned. "Dude, it means if we find anything gold."

"Oh, okay . . . let's try it out."

Juliann passed back the metal detector and they walked behind the Bright Lite. "It's quite heavy, isn't it?" said Alex, wondering whether it really was heavy or he was just sore.

Juliann ignored his question. "We've got to be systematic," she said. "My dad always says that. He's an engineer and he says you can't find anything or do anything properly if you don't take a 'systematic approach.'"

"Okay," agreed Alex. "So how far out shall we search?"

"Seriously, dude, the marsh is right over there!" She pointed and shuddered noticeably. "I may like spiders and iguanas, but I don't fancy meeting alligators or poisonous snakes!"

"All right, so we have to stay around the grassy area behind the Bright Lite."

"Let's walk up and down in straight lines," Juliann suggested. "We'll start here." She pushed the spade into the ground to mark their starting point.

They swept the metal detector from side to side while they walked. They walked, and walked some more, over short grass and through long grass, but away from the bulrushes of the marsh. After an hour with not one 'hit', Alex was feeling really down.

"Are you sure this thing works?" he asked, wiping his forehead with the sleeve of his T-shirt.

"Positive."

"Then why hasn't it picked up anything?"

"Because there's nothing that's gold under here!"

He sighed. "Do you want to keep going?"

"Sure," said Juliann. "Here, I'll have a go."

Alex lagged behind, drinking water as Juliann walked up and down, sweeping the contraption from side to side. "It makes your arms ache, doesn't it?" she commented.

"Yeah, and you don't have the bruises that I do," said Alex, feeling vindicated.

Suddenly there was a crackling sound. "We've found something!" shouted Juliann. "Look! Look at the display!"

"Don't lose the place," Alex shouted as he ran and grabbed the spade.

His heart was racing as he started shoveling the soil. This was it—the moment he had waited for. He was about to find Cabeza de Vaca's treasure. He dug deeper and deeper until he saw something glinting. "I see it! I see it!" he shouted, throwing down the spade and falling on his knees next to the hole.

He fought the pain in his leg, leaned in and pulled out the gold object. It was much smaller than he expected and partially covered in dirt, so he rubbed it off on his shirt. His heart sank—it wasn't a gold coin at all.

"Ewww! Gross!" said Juliann, pulling a face.

"Why is it gross?" asked Alex.

"Dude, don't you know what that is?"

Alex shook his head.

"It's a gold crown from someone's mouth—dentists put those over a bad tooth!"

Alex wasn't fazed. "Well, it's not our treasure, but it still might be worth something." He slipped it into his pocket.

"So do we keep trying?"

Alex had already picked up the metal detector and had started to search again. "You bet. At least now we know this thing works."

Two hours later, the sun was getting high. Alex was dripping with sweat. Juliann still looked cool and perfect in her pink outfit. He didn't know how she could still look that good after hours of searching in the heat. They had covered the entire area around the Bright Lite and found nothing else in that whole time.

"I have to stop," said Alex.

"You giving up?" Juliann asked.

"Nah. I just need to take a break."

"How about an ice cream? Want one?"

"Sure," said Alex. "I'll stay down here with the metal detector."

"Why don't you walk across China Clipper Drive and sit in the shade?" she suggested.

"Great idea," he replied.

Alex crossed the narrow street, and lay on the grass in the shade next to the neighborhood mailboxes. He looked at the metal detector with contempt. "Stupid thing!" he grumbled.

He gave it a kick with his foot, wanting to take his frustration out on something, but hurt his bruised leg in the process. Suddenly the machine came to life, crackling as loudly as before.

"Dang it!" Alex jumped to his feet, feeling really guilty. Had he broken the metal detector? His father would kill him! Juliann's father would kill him! How much did these things cost?

He picked it up and examined it to see what damage he had done. It seemed okay, but it was still making that annoying crackling noise. He looked at the display on the handle and saw that it was indicating gold right where he was standing!

He hadn't broken it! He must have accidently kicked the 'on' button. Gold! There was more gold—right where he was standing!

Juliann was running towards him with a dripping ice cream in each hand. "Has the metal detector found something else?"

"I think so! Get over here!" said Alex, hardly able to contain his excitement.

"Here!" She thrust an ice cream at him. "Eat it quickly!"

Alex had never eaten anything so cold, so fast. He took a huge bite and then stuffed the rest into his mouth. The cream ran down his chin. He licked his fingers and rubbed his hands down his pants.

Juliann handed him the spade and yelled, "Start digging! What are you waiting for?"

The ground was hard, as if it had been baked in an oven, but he wasn't about to let that stop him. Taking off the grass to reach the soil below was hard enough, but after a few minutes it seemed as though he had only scratched the surface. Boy, was this ever hard work!

"Come on, Alex," Juliann encouraged. "You can do it!"

Six inches . . . nine inches. How much farther? He stopped and took a deep breath.

"It's got to be down there," said Juliann. "Something has to be down there! Keep going!"

Three inches more, and then another three . . . the hole *had* to be over a foot deep. Where was the gold?

Then Alex heard the spade hit metal. He froze. This was it. He didn't want to be disappointed again. "Do you think it will be another gold crown?" he asked.

Juliann was jumping up and down. "How do I know? Just get it out of there!" she screamed at him.

Alex dropped the spade and groveled in the hole. First he pulled out a piece of black leather cord. His heart beat faster. Could it be? Could it really be? He tucked it into his pocket and clawed at the bottom of the hole with his fingernails. He felt the metal. It was something round.

He stood up slowly, peering at what was in his hands and hardly daring to believe what he had found. His heart felt like it would explode. It was a coin . . . a gold coin, for sure. It was about the size of a quarter, worn at the edges, with a strange eight-pointed shape on one side, and the head of a man and a lady in the center of the other side. There were letters around the edges on both sides.

"Dude!" said Juliann, leaning in to take a look. "Is that what I think it is?"

Alex swallowed hard. "Unreal. Totally unreal," he said. "I can read the letters C-A-R, and there's a number—15-something, I think."

"But is it a Spanish coin?"

"Dunno," said Alex.

"Are there any more down there?" asked Juliann.

Alex passed her the coin. "Don't drop it!" he ordered. Once again he was down on his knees, scraping in the dirt. "Yes!" he screamed. "There's another one!"

He studied the second coin and then passed it to her. It was almost the same as the first, but not in such good condition.

"There may be more," he said, continuing to scrape the bottom of the hole with his fingers, but this time he came up empty handed. He stood up and brushed himself down. "I think that's it for this hole, but I'll bet you anything there's a whole lot more around here!"

Juliann swept the metal detector in circles around them. It crackled continuously. "This is a gold mine beneath our feet!"

"Geez," said Alex. "The machine is going crazy! We've found Cabeza de Vaca's treasure! We've really found it!"

"So shall we keep digging?"

Alex shook his head. He was dripping with sweat and exhausted—and his leg hurt more than ever. But even if he wanted to carry on and uncover more treasure, he knew he couldn't—not until he knew what to do with it. "I can't," he told Juliann. "I just can't do anymore today."

Juliann turned off the machine and laid it on the ground. "Wait until everyone finds out about this!" she said, taking out her cell phone.

Alex suddenly felt sick. "Stop! Don't do that! You can't tell anyone—not yet!"

"Why not?"

"Because I have to figure out what to do with the gold. Remember the rhyme: 'What you find, leave behind on my sweet San Luis Isle,'" said Alex. "I promised him. I promised the ghost of Cabeza de Vaca that the treasure wouldn't leave the island."

Juliann looked pale and handed the coins back to him. "I think you'd better keep your promise to a ghost," she said. "You wouldn't want to be haunted forever, would you?"

"Thanks a lot," said Alex. "You're not helping. You're making me nervous. But what am I supposed to do? Should I put them back in the hole?"

"Call Suzan!" said Juliann. "She'll know what to do."

Chapter 17

Suzan's silver car pulled up next to the Treasure Island mailboxes on China Clipper Drive. Alex couldn't believe how fast she had got there—Juliann had called her only twelve minutes ago. She opened the car door and walked at speed toward them. Alex could see the excitement all over her face.

Suzan said nothing until she was standing beside them. "You really found some gold coins?" she asked quietly.

"Yes, ma'am! Cabeza de Vaca's treasure," whispered Alex, opening his fist and showing her the two coins in his sweaty palm. "And according to the metal detector, there's a whole lot more down there."

She picked one up and examined it. "Well, I'm no coin expert, but they do look like gold, and they're definitely very old. We'll take them to Michael and Jamie, and they'll find a coin expert who can tell us about them."

"I can't do that," said Alex.

Suzan gave him a quizzical look. "We can sort out later whether you have the right to claim them," she said. "But we ought to find out how old they are and if they're valuable."

"No, you don't get it," said Juliann. "It's nothing to do with Alex wanting to keep them. The coins can't go to the museum in Angleton."

"I'm sorry—I don't understand," said Suzan.

"I saw the ghost of Cabeza de Vaca again last night," said Alex. "He gave me a warning."

"A warning?"

"It's really spooked him," said Juliann, "and it's spooked me too."

"What did he say this time?" asked Suzan.

"He said, 'Help me rest, help me go. Find what's buried on Malhado. But what you find, leave behind on my sweet San Luis Isle.'"

"So now you're scared to let the coins go to Angleton because it means they will leave the island?" asked Suzan.

Alex nodded. "What am I supposed to do? He wanted me to find the gold coins, but I can't let them leave the island."

Suzan touched him gently on the shoulder. "You have to consider that these coins might not be Spanish, and probably have nothing to do with Cabeza de Vaca."

"I *know* they do," said Alex firmly. "This is some of Cabeza de Vaca's treasure, I'm sure of it. And I'm certain there's more buried around here." He turned in circles. "The metal detector said so."

"Enough to fill a brown pouch?" asked Suzan.

Alex smiled.

"Okay, so we need to come up with a plan—something that you are comfortable with," said Suzan. "What you find, leave behind," she muttered.

"He could keep them at Island Sapphire," said Juliann.

"Yeah, right," said Alex. "They might be really valuable. Mom and Dad would want them straight in a vault or in a museum."

Suzan's face lit up. "That's it!" she said. "We'll take them to The Village of Surfside Beach Museum! That way they won't leave the island, and they'll be in a glass case where everyone can enjoy them."

Alex felt elated. "That's a great idea!"

"So you think your ghost would approve?"

"Yes, ma'am!" said Alex.

Chapter 18

Alex stared through the glass cabinet at the two gold coins. It had been a long day, but he was thrilled with the outcome. The museum was organizing an official dig to recover any more buried coins.

Suzan came up behind. "So, you were right, Alex," she said. "Our local coin expert says that the two coins are rare Spanish coins, and they are very valuable!"

"Really?" questioned Alex, turning to talk to her.

"He thinks that they are Catalonian principats. The C-A-R stands for Carlos I who became Charles V of Spain. The heads on the coins are of Charles V and Joanna, his mother, and the numerals 1 and 5 that you saw are the beginning of the date of the coin —1521."

"1521? I knew it!" said Alex. "Cabeza de Vaca landed on San Luis Island in 1528, which means that the coins *are* from his time period. I told you—I found Cabeza de Vaca's treasure!"

Suzan grinned at him. "Alex, there'll never be any proof that he buried the coins when he was here in 1528, or that Alex Glass Follett found them again in 1840, or that Cabeza de Vaca's ghost told you to find his treasure."

"But *I* know, and the ghost of Cabeza de Vaca knows," said Alex. "And that's good enough for me."

"Well, then, I'm glad that you're happy with the outcome," said Suzan. "I've certainly learned a lot of local history through your experiences, and now I shall always wonder about ghosts."

"Ma'am, you mean that you're still not convinced that I saw the ghost of Cabeza de Vaca?"

Suzan smiled at him. "I'm keeping an open mind," she replied. "By the way . . . you've got press and TV interviews arranged for this evening—we'd better get home and tell your parents the exciting news. I'm going to the car with Juliann. See you outside in a minute."

Alex took one last look around the upstairs room of City Hall, which temporarily housed The Village of Surfside Beach Museum. They were building a new museum and the curator had promised that Cabeza de Vaca's gold coins would be on display when it opened.

Alex pulled the thin piece of leather cord out of his pocket. He knew it was all that was left of Cabeza de Vaca's pouch. "This is the proof," he said to himself.

As Alex walked down the old wooden stairs he heard a whisper.

"Thank you, Alexander Glassssssssssss."

Top: The entrance to Treasure Island, San Luis Pass, Texas
Bottom: The footbridge to Treasure Island's beautiful beach

Top: The Telephone Exchange at the entrance to Treasure Island

Bottom: The Bright Lite, Treasure Island, San Luis Pass, Texas
Owned by Don Bright since 1983, managed by Debbie Broadway

Top: The Brazoria County Historical Museum, Angleton, Texas
Bottom: City Hall, Surfside Beach, which houses The Village of
Surfside Beach Museum

Part 11

The Real Story
of Malhado-
San Luis Island, Texas

The Real Story of Malhado

Cabeza de Vaca and Malhado (San Luis Island, Texas)

Álvar Núñez Cabeza de Vaca – public domain image

Álvar Núñez Cabeza de Vaca was born in 1490 into a wealthy Spanish family. His ancestors had been warriors for generations. Cabeza de Vaca's name means "head of a cow." This title was given by Spain's king to one of Cabeza de Vaca's ancestors, who aided the king's men during battle by cleverly marking a difficult trail with cow skulls. The king's men were able to find their way and, as a consequence, the king was victorious in battle.

In early 1527 Cabeza de Vaca joined a royal expedition of 600 men led by Governor Narváez of Spain. The idea behind the expedition was to occupy North America.

Just off the shore of Cuba their fleet was battered by a hurricane. After obtaining a new boat, they finally reached Florida in 1528 near what we now call Tampa Bay.

Narváez then made a disastrous decision to divide his forces into two: one for land and the other for sea. Cabeza de Vaca begged him not to leave the ships unprotected in the bay in the unsettled country. He feared that they would never again see the ships or the men who had stayed with them.

The Ghosts of Malhado

He was right. Cabeza de Vaca spent most of that year trudging through Florida in search of food and riches. He never did locate the ships.

The Apalachee Indians of Florida pursued the men relentlessly through swampy terrain, hiding behind trees and showering them with arrows. The group fought off the Indians for months. Many men and horses were wounded, and their guide was captured.

Cabeza de Vaca, the governor, and the remaining men suffered from disease and malnutrition. In order to survive, they lived off the flesh of their horses.

By the end of that year, the men were desperate, and they knew they had to leave Florida to survive. They made some bellows from deer hide to make a fire hot enough to forge nails and tools. They melted down horseshoes, stirrups and spurs, and using horsehides and trees they built five primitive boats, each with room for only 50 men. With Cabeza de Vaca commanding one of these vessels, they set off in search of Cuba.

They followed the coast westward until they reached the mouth of the Mississippi River. But the strong current swept them into the gulf and tragedy hit once again. The small fleet was separated by another hurricane, and some of the boats were lost at sea, including that of Narváez.

By the time the hurricane blew Cabeza de Vaca and his companions ashore, thirst, starvation and storms had whittled their numbers to only 80. The storm dumped them on the Gulf Coast of Texas at San Luis Island. It was November 6, 1528.

This is an extract from *The Journey of Alvar Nuñez Cabeza de Vaca*, written by Cabeza de Vaca in 1542, and translated by Fanny Bandelier in 1905:

"Close to shore a wave took us and hurled the barge a horse's length out of water. With the violent shock nearly all the people who lay in the boat like dead came to themselves, and, seeing we were close to land, began to crawl out on all fours. As they took to some rocks, we built a fire and toasted some of our maize. We found rain water, and with the warmth of the fire, people revived and began to cheer up. The day we arrived there was the sixth of the month of November."

Cabeza de Vaca named the island La Isla de Malhado, which translated means the Island of Ill-Fate or the Island of Bad Luck.

According to Cabeza de Vaca's journal, after everyone had eaten he sent one of his strongest men, Lope de Oviedo, to climb to the top of the nearest tree to see where they were and what the surroundings were like.

Oviedo reported back that they were on an island. Cabeza de Vaca sent him off a second time to follow any worn trails. This time Oviedo discovered Indian huts, empty because the Indians were out in the fields. He stole a cooking pot and a few other items. Three Indians with bows and arrows followed him back, calling to him. Not long after, one hundred archers joined them on the beach.

At the sight of the Indians, Cabeza de Vaca was frightened. Only three of the Spaniards had the energy to stand upright after their ordeal at sea. He realized that they could not possibly fight off so many Indians, so they tried to save themselves by giving the Indians beads and bells. In return, one of the Indians gave him an arrow as a sign of friendship.

Using sign language to communicate with the Indians, Cabeza de Vaca understood that the Indians would return the following day with food . . . and they did. As they had promised, they arrived at sunrise with fish, and roots that tasted like nuts.

Cabeza de Vaca's journal tells us about life on the island . . .

"To this island we gave the name of the Island of Ill-Fate. The people on it are tall and well formed; they have no other weapons than bows and arrows with which they are most dexterous. . . The women do the hard work. People stay on this island from October till the end of February, feeding on the roots I have mentioned, taken from under the water in November and December. They have channels made of reeds and get fish only during that time; afterwards they subsist on roots. At the end of February they remove to other parts in search of food, because the roots begin to sprout and are not good anymore."

Cabeza de Vaca 1542

To begin with, Cabeza de Vaca and his friends were welcomed by the native Karankawa Indians on San Luis Island, but soon the weather turned cold and the Indians were no longer able to pull roots. To make matters worse, they seemed unable to catch any fish either.

One by one Cabeza de Vaca's men died, until only 15 were left. Then the Karankawa Indians fell sick from a stomach ailment, and half of them also died. They blamed Cabeza de Vaca for the deaths and agreed amongst themselves that the 15 Spaniards should be killed.

Fortunately, one Indian argued that if the white man had so much power, then why had he been unable to prevent his own people from dying? And so they were spared.

Cabeza de Vaca took seriously ill and became separated from the other survivors of the expedition. They believed that he had died on the mainland, and so, in 1529 they set off down the coast without him. Also left behind on San Luis Island was Lope de Oviedo.

Cabeza de Vaca recovered from near death. He continued to live among the Indians and became the first European trader in Texas.

The Indians allowed him to come and go, trading sea shells and mesquite beans from the coast for skins and red ochre from the tribes inland. Red ochre was considered a very valuable commodity by the Indians as it was used to paint their bodies.

The Indians also considered Cabeza de Vaca to be a medicine man since he prayed over the sick and even breathed on their injuries.

It was not until 1532 that Cabeza de Vaca persuaded Lope de Oviedo to leave San Luis Island and accompany him south to Panuco, Mexico, following the route of the earlier survivors. But Lope turned back, and he is never mentioned again in any historical record.

Cabeza de Vaca carried on alone and, amazingly, managed to meet up with three other survivors—Alonso del Castillo Maldonando, Andrés Dorantes de Carranca, and Estevan, an African slave—at what they called "the river of nuts." We now believe that "the river of nuts" was the Guadalupe River.

By the end of 1532 these four men were the only remaining survivors of the original Narváez expedition and had become slaves to the Mariame Indians.

Although the men constantly plotted an escape, it was not until 1534 that they finally managed to slip away. They headed west, traveling across what is now Texas and into Mexico.

In July 1536 they finally met up with a group of their countrymen in Mexico on a slave-taking expedition. The Spaniards were taken aback at the sight of Cabeza de Vaca wearing hardly anything. In his journal, Cabeza de Vaca remembers the meeting:

"dumbfounded at the sight of me, strangely dressed and in the company of Indians. They just stood staring for a long time."

Cabeza de Vaca spent four years living on San Luis Island and at least another four years wandering around Texas. You could say that he was the first geographer and historian in Texas. He is the only person ever to have lived among the coastal Indians of Texas—and to have survived to write about them.

The Next Three Hundred Years

Karankawa Indians–public domain image

The history of San Luis Island is vague until the mid-1800's. We do know that it was inhabited by the Karankawa Indians, who were excellent fishermen, hunters and archers.

The Karankawa were between six and seven feet tall, and were known for painting and tattooing their bodies. They had bows almost as tall as they were, and their long arrows were made from slender shoots of cane. The men waded in the shallow waters with lances to spear fish, while women and children searched for blue crabs, oysters and shellfish. They also harvested nuts and berries.

The Karankawa were a nomadic people that lived mainly around the bays along the Gulf Coast. They built wikiups, which were huts made out of animal skins, and traveled around mostly by canoe or on foot. It is said that they were the fiercest Indians on the Coastal Plains.

By 1824 the white man had chased off the Karankawas and the tribe had all but disappeared.

San Luis Island and the Follett Family

John Bradbury Follett

Anne Louise Fownes Follett

Pictures courtesy of Brazoria County Historical Museum

180

The exciting history of San Luis Island really began in 1839 when the city of San Luis was founded.

In 1832, when San Luis Pass was surveyed, it was discovered that the water was 18 feet deep, which was deep enough for large sailing ships to easily pass through.

George L. Hammeken from Philadelphia envisioned a great port on San Luis Island that would rival New Orleans. He convinced investors to put up the money.

Just as Treasure Island's beautiful coastline attracts both vacationers and new residents today, settlers in the 1840's were drawn by the images in Hammeken's brochures, which portrayed San Luis as a paradise. People came from as far away as France and England, and many arrived believing that they were coming to a lush tropical paradise. They were then disappointed when they arrived to find only a small sandy knoll.

The Folletts were one of those families who chose to make San Luis Island their new home. The Folletts were an exceptional family who added so much to our Texas history. In fact, the island south of Galveston is now known as Follett's Island.

John Bradbury Follett was originally from New Hampshire. He had been an apprentice to a shipbuilder in Canada from an early age. He and his wife, Anne Louise Fownes, had eight children.

In 1838 Follett came to Galveston looking to buy land to build a shipyard in the new republic. Soon after, the family moved to Galveston and started repairing and building boats.

When the city of San Luis was founded in 1839, the family sold their home and moved their business across the pass to the thriving new town. The first recorded history of the area shows John Bradbury owning Lots 3 and 4 in Block 22 First Ward in the City of San Luis. See if you can find this on the map of San Luis. (Clue: look for the big number 1, and then find block 22.)

Forty houses were built almost immediately, and in less than five years the population had reached 2,000. San Luis was home to many eminent residents, including doctors, scientists and politicians.

By 1840 the town had two general stores, a portrait painter, a land office, and the *San Luis Advocate* newspaper, and even two hotels. The town's cotton compress was the first built in Texas. A mule, walking in a circle, turned the huge wooden screw that pressed the cotton into bales. Cisterns were built with Philadelphia bricks to catch and hold fresh water to supply the new town.

Below are three advertisements that appeared in the *San Luis Advocate* in 1840:

To Mill Wrights and Carpenters

WANTED to contract with a first rate workman to erect a **WIND MILL** for the grinding of corn in San Luis city to be built in a neat and substantial manner and according to plans and specifications which will be exhibited.

Apply to CHAS G. BRYANT

San Luis, Aug 26 1840

BENNETT'S HOTEL
SAN LUIS, BRAZORIA CO.

The subscriber has opened his house for the accommodation of Travelers and Boarders.

CHARLES H BENNETT

BOOKS, PAMPHLETS, & C
Executed at the shortest notice and best style at the
office of THE SAN LUIS ADVOCATE
CORNER OF MARKET & LIBERTY STS
SAN LUIS, TX

In August 1840 the San Luis wharf was built. It was 1,000 feet long! Large warehouses were built alongside the wharf, and it is said that as many as 10 ships were in the harbor at one time. In 1841 over 5,000 bales of cotton were shipped from the San Luis wharf, destined either for New England or Europe.

A mule-drawn ferry regularly crossed the pass to Galveston Island. According to an advertisement in the *San Luis Advocate* on October 30, 1840, tickets cost:

62 cents per person
$1.37 for a man and a horse
$2 for a man and a wagon
$1.50 per head for cattle.

But the bustling city of San Luis eventually died. Because of severe storms the harbor began to silt up, making it dangerous for ships to enter the port. The depression of 1840 took its toll on the residents, and people began to leave. Many storms and hurricanes destroyed buildings and homes.

By 1883 only 400 of the 2,000 residents remained and, after the great hurricane of 1900, the city of San Luis ceased to exist.

Once again San Luis Island lived up to its earlier name, Malhado.

The original plan of the City of San Luis. The hand-written inscription underneath it reads: I certify the foregoing to be the correct plan of the city of San Luis situated on the Island of San Luis as surveyed by me. Brazoria 1st October 1841

William Henry Austin, Civil Engineer

Plan courtesy of Brazoria County Historical Museum

John Bradbury Follett died in 1846 at age 51, but his wife and sons stayed on San Luis Island. They moved house and, in 1847, Alonzo, Joseph and Alexander Glass Follett constructed the famous Half Way House. Mrs. Bradbury Follett served meals and offered lodging to weary travelers between Velasco (now part of Surfside Beach) and Galveston.

Picture courtesy of Brazoria County Historical Commission

This was a grand colonial house, three stories high, with 15 rooms and open galleries on each floor. Oleanders grew all around the house. They were said to be so tall that they reached the third floor. Some years later when the Hades House was built, bricks with a Philadelphia imprint were unearthed. This helped to pinpoint the location of the Folletts' Half Way House.

Half Way House was damaged several times during storms but even after the huge storm in 1854, when many more residents packed up and left San Luis, the Folletts rebuilt Half Way House and kept it open. In fact the house was open for 50 years and was finally destroyed by the great hurricane that also demolished Galveston in 1900.

Anne Follett placed this advertisement in a Brazoria newspaper, *The Texas Planter*, on August 23, 1854:

SAN LUIS.

The subscriber has opened an establishment for the entertainment of travelers at the West Pass. Horse feed always on hand. Mrs. Follett

---

But the Folletts contributed so much more to San Luis Island than just Half Way House. They operated a ferry service, which was also a mail service, across Big Pass (now called San Luis Pass). They also operated boats across Little Pass, the stretch of water that once separated San Luis Island from mainland Brazoria County, where Treasure Island is today. The Follett family also raised cattle, and grew many crops and owned two sailboats to ship their produce.

You may have heard of the *Lafitte,* the first steam boat built in Texas. John Bradbury Follett and his sons built the boat on the mouth of the Brazos River, where Surfside Beach is today.

The *Lafitte* was named after the French pirate Jean Lafitte, who helped the Republic of Texas in its war for independence from Mexico.

Alexander Glass Follett, the fourth child of the Folletts, was born in 1823. When the Civil War broke out, he signed up and served under General Bates for the Confederacy. He was even captured and held for a time on a Yankee gun boat off San Luis Pass! Alexander often wrote for both the *Galveston Tribune* and the *Galveston News.* He died in Velasco, now Surfside Beach, in 1906.

San Luis Island Today

Today San Luis Island is part of Follett's Island. San Luis Island was once cut off by the waters of Cold Pass which emptied into the gulf through two cuts. The cuts were known as Little Pass and Big Pass, which was renamed San Luis Pass. But over the years Big Pass and Little Pass filled up with silt until San Luis was no longer an island.

These days you can reach Galveston Island easily. Instead of having to take a ferry across San Luis Pass there is a beautiful bridge which takes just a few minutes to drive across.

The San Luis Pass Vacek bridge was opened in December 1966. It only costs $2 to drive across today. Compare that with $2 for a man and his wagon 170 years ago! Not everything has increased in price!

Treasure Island Municipal District was set up in 1967, right at the eastern tip of Follett's Island, where San Luis Island was once located. As the population grew in the 1970's it became obvious that there was a need for a general store and a gas station. Mr. Tom Bright believed that Treasure Island would continue to prosper and so he built the Bright Lite, a general store selling everything from food and hardware to general merchandise, and even bait and tackle.

In 1983 a mighty hurricane, Alicia, leveled his store but, just as the Folletts had done a century before, Mr. Bright rebuilt. Now his store, owned by his son Don Bright, is the center of the community of Treasure Island and residents often hold their meetings there. Today there are only about 25 permanent residents in Treasure Island but many more come and go, visiting their beach houses throughout the year. They always leave with sadness and long for their next visit to

Malhado.

San Luis Island Timeline

1528	Cabeza de Vaca lands November 6th and calls the island Malhado
1532	Cabeza de Vaca escapes from the Coastal Indians
1500's –1824	Karankawa Indians inhabit the island
1838	The Folletts move to Galveston
1839	City of San Luis founded
1839	The Folletts arrive in San Luis
1840	The Depression begins to affect San Luis
1846	John Bradbury Follett dies
1847	Anne Follett and three sons construct Half Way House
1861	Alexander Glass Follett joins the Confederacy
1883	Only 400 residents remain in San Luis
1886	(Approx) Cold Pass fills with silt and San Luis Island becomes San Luis Peninsula
1900	The Great Hurricane destroys Half Way House
1967	Treasure Island is founded on San Luis Peninsula
1970	Tom Bright builds the Bright Lite General Store

1983	Hurricane Alicia destroys the Bright Lite but Mr. Bright rebuilds.
2008	Hurricane Ike causes damage to Treasure Island and the entire coast of Follett's Island.

Part III

Where was
San Luis Island,
Texas ?

Where was San Luis Island?

The state map of Texas showing the location of
San Luis Island

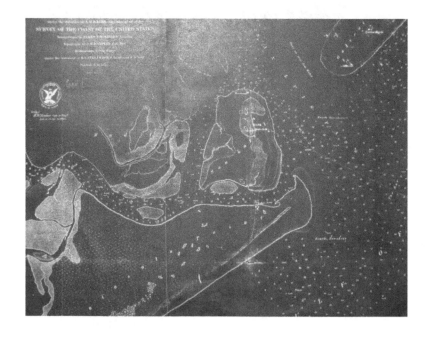

Courtesy of Brazoria County Historical Museum

You can clearly see on the 1853 survey that San Luis Island was separated from Peninsula Point by Cold Water Pass and from Galveston Island by San Luis Pass. Today, because of hurricanes changing the landscape and silt from the surrounding waters filling up the Pass, it has now become part of Follett's Island. San Luis Island is no more.

Follett's Island and Galveston Island are separated by San Luis Pass. The community of Treasure Island is located in San Luis Pass at the tip of Follett's Island.

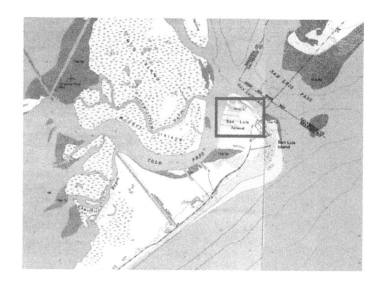

Key Map courtesy of Brazoria County Historical Museum

The red square shows the original location of San Luis Island. Today this is the neighborhood of Treasure Island in San Luis Pass, and also the location of San Luis Pass County Park.

The Malhado Debate

For many years people have argued about the real location of Malhado in Texas. Some have said that it was Galveston Island, and others have said as far south as Port Aransas.

In 1897 Bethel Coopwood was the first to pinpoint Cabeza de Vaca's landing on San Luis Island, in Brazoria County, Texas. But even in a court case in 1990, people were still saying that Malhado was really Galveston Island. The court ruled that the argument for Galveston Island was unconvincing.

Cabeza de Vaca described the island where he landed as being one-half league wide by 5 leagues long (1.3 miles wide by 13 miles long). That is far too small to be Galveston Island, which is 3 miles wide and 27 miles long. We know that Spaniards in the 1500's were very accurate with their measurements, so it is unlikely that Cabeza de Vaca would have been so wrong.

In his personal account of his adventures, Cabeza de Vaca also describes quite vividly the landscape and the plants growing on La Isla de Malhado. According to scientific studies these characteristics match up with San Luis Island. Cabeza de Vaca does mention a large island *behind* Malhado, lying toward Florida. We now believe that this island behind Malhado is Galveston Island.

And From the Demons Hide
Treasure Island, Texas

Four hundred years of history
De Vaca to Follett
Malhado once but now no more
It's bad luck men forget
And too this island's Indians
Karankawas six feet tall
There feasted on the common man
As cannibals one and all
Recorded in world history
The only incident
Then every native disappeared
The white man's precedent
Still old San Luis stayed a dream
Of a Philadelphia man
With John Follett great shipyards came
Atop the sugar sand
The island ferries serviced them
Both passes to the sea
The Big and too the Little one
To cross would take a fee
With ferry boats and cattlemen
Velasco prospered well
But when the harbor ghosts appeared
It was a living hell
As monsters rising midst the sand

In Hades House reside
Its residents did stow their fears
And from these demons hide
Yet still through years four eighty two
This Island has survived
Though Jean LaFitte's great treasure trove
Might only be contrived
And though his pirates disappeared
Marauding through the night
God blesses us and everyone
If spirits are in sight

David Devaney
09-24-2010

David Devaney is very familiar with the Texas Gulf Coast. For 10 years he has been traveling the pirates' route from Galveston, across San Luis Pass, to Treasure Island and then through to Surfside. He often fished from the San Luis pier, before it was destroyed by Hurricane Ike, and he works for the company that owns the Pirate's Alley Café in Surfside Beach.

David lives in Houston and writes poetry every day for his five grandchildren and for his own enjoyment. He has been writing poetry since he was a young man of 17 in Pennsylvania, and he intends to retire to Surfside Beach on Follett's Island, Texas.

Sources

Books

Alvar Nuñez Cabeza de Vaca, *The Journey of Alvar Nuñez Cabeza De Vaca*. First published as La Relacion (1542) and then later as Naufragios. Translated by Fanny Bandelier (1905).

Turner Publishing Company, *Daughters of the Republic of Texas, Volume I. Patriot Ancestor Album*, Page 98, John Bradbury Follett and Alexander Glass Follett.

Maps/Plans/Photographs

Plan of City of San Luis 1841, courtesy of Brazoria County Historical Museum.

Plat Map – Treasure Island Section 2 (San Luis Island) 2009.025c.0001 Map courtesy of Brazoria County Historical Museum.

San Luis Pass, Texas: Survey of the Coast of the United States, Published in 1853, courtesy of Brazoria County Historical Museum.

Drawing of the Follett's Half Way House, courtesy of the Brazoria County Historical Commission.

Photographs of John Bradbury Follett and Anne Louise Fownes Follett, courtesy of Brazoria County Historical Museum.

Articles

Vaugn, Donna. "Young Seaport Short Lived," *The Brazosport Facts*, July 27, 1986.

Phinny, Nann C. "San Luis Synonymous with bad luck," *The Brazosport Facts*, July 22, 1979.

No author credited. "Span rises on site of Obliterated San Luis City," *The Brazosport Facts*, Dec. 16, 1966.

No author credited. "Seamen Built it to Buck Gales," *The Brazosport Facts*, Dec. 16, 1966.

Copies of advertisements from the *San Luis Advocate* 1840

Websites

Treasure Island, Texas: The History of Treasure Island
http://www.treasureislandtx.org/index.htm

Museum of South Texas History:
http://www.mosthistory.org/

The Handbook of Texas Online: Malhado Island

http://www.tshaonline.org/handbook/online/articles/M
M/rrm1.html

PBS New perspectives on The West: Alvar Nuñez Cabeza de
Vaca
http://www.pbs.org/weta/thewest/people/a_c/cabezadev
aca.htm

The University of Texas at Austin: Learning from Cabeza de
Vaca http://www.texasbeyondhistory.net

People Talk to Ghosts in their Sleep: Impact Lab
http://www.impactlab.net/2007/07/05/people-talk-to-
ghosts-in-their-sleep/

Hurricane Preparedness: Hurricane History
http://www.nhc.noaa.gov/HAW2/english/history.shtml#i
ke

University of Texas Libraries, Perry-Castañeda Library Map
Collection http://www.lib.utexas.edu/maps/faq.html

Photo by the Tribune Newspaper, Humble, Texas

About the Author

H.J. Ralles is a teacher who turned to writing books for children in 1997. Originally from the United Kingdom, H.J. Ralles has lived in the United States since 1990. She now lives in Huffman, Texas. She is the author of the popular *Keeper* series and three other science fiction novels for 9- to 14-year-olds. *The Ghosts of Malhado* is her ninth book.

To learn more about H.J. Ralles visit:
www.hjralles.com